Alison Roberts lives in Christchurch, New Zealand, and has written over 60 Mills & Boon® Medical Romances™. As a qualified paramedic, she has personal experience of the drama and emotion to be found in the world of medical professionals, and loves to weave stories with this rich background—especially when they can have a happy ending. When Alison is not writing, you'll find her indulging her passion for dancing or spending time with her friends (including Molly the dog) and her daughter Becky, who has grown up to become a brilliant artist. She also loves to travel, hates housework, and considers it a triumph when the flowers outnumber the weeds in her garden.

Recent titles by Alison Roberts:

NYC ANGELS: AN EXPLOSIVE REUNION~
ST PIRAN'S: THE WEDDING!†
MAYBE THIS CHRISTMAS…?
THE LEGENDARY PLAYBOY SURGEON**
FALLING FOR HER IMPOSSIBLE BOSS**
SYDNEY HARBOUR HOSPITAL: ZOE'S BABY*
ST PIRAN'S: THE BROODING HEART SURGEON†

~NYC Angels
**Heartbreakers of St Patrick's Hospital
*Sydney Harbour Hospital
†St Piran's Hospital

Tom could clearly see the wave of relief in her eyes as she registered the bright uniforms of the helicopter crew. And then he saw the shock as she caught his gaze.

As she recognised him.

'Oh, my God…*Tom*…?'

The shock was mutual. Tom had thought that being on an island in the aftermath of a massive earthquake was the last thing he'd be expected to have to deal with.

But he'd been so wrong.

Seeing Abby again was…was such a shock he couldn't even begin to process it.

That hair, with its gorgeous golden honey colour and the length that made it so damn sexy when it brushed on naked skin…

Her voice…

Those huge blue eyes that darkened in colour if her mood was extreme. They were as dark as he'd ever seen them right now. She was shocked. Afraid.

Dear Reader

I live in Christchurch, New Zealand, and on the 22nd February 2011 our city suffered a catastrophic earthquake. As a paramedic, I was privileged to be within the Red Zone in the early hours and days, but people the world over soon became aware of the heroism of our emergency services like firemen, police officers, paramedics and USAR teams. And not only the professionals. Many of our heroes were ordinary people who just happened to be thrown into extraordinary circumstances.

Disasters bring out the best in the vast majority of people, and I've learned that they can have some other interesting effects. The rate of deaths from heart attacks increases, for instance, but it's balanced by an uncannily similar increase in births. People make big decisions, too, especially about relationships, as the reminder of how precious life is makes us realise what's really important. I heard of many people who made a lifelong commitment to each other in the wake of the Christchurch earthquake.

Marion Lennox and I didn't set our *Earthquake!* duet in Christchurch, for obvious reasons, but we were drawn to explore the emotional repercussions of a natural disaster.

My people, Abby and Tom, certainly needed something earth-shattering to get them back together and make sure it works this time.

I have every confidence that they will have a very happy future.

I hope you'll agree :-)

Happy Reading!

With love

Alison xxx

MIRACLE ON KAIMOTU ISLAND by Marion Lennox
is also available this month
from Mills & Boon® Medical Romance™

ALWAYS
THE HERO

BY
ALISON ROBERTS

MILLS
BOON™

First published in Great Britain 2013
by Mills & Boon, an imprint of Harlequin (UK) Limited.
Harlequin (UK) Limited, Eton House, 18-24 Paradise Road,
Richmond, Surrey TW9 1SR

© Alison Roberts 2013

ISBN: 978 0 263 23372 8

CHAPTER ONE

'WHAT'S SO INTERESTING out there, Abby?'

'Nothing.' Abigail Miller jerked her gaze away from the window, sending an apologetic smile to the young woman who'd asked the question.

It wasn't a completely truthful response. There was a lot to be seen out of the window of this consulting room in Kaimotu Island's medical centre. The modern building that housed the consulting rooms and surgical facilities was attached to the old wooden cottage hospital that had been built many years ago on a prime piece of land.

Being on top of a hill, they had one of the best views—encompassing the township where most of the permanent community lived and the small, sheltered harbour against a backdrop that had ragged bush-covered slopes created by an ancient volcano on one side and a seemingly endless ocean on the other.

She could see a gorgeous, fresh-out-of-the-box April autumn day for one thing, with the intense blue of the sky only surpassed by the deeper blue of the sea. A stunning stretch of golden sand on a beach bordered by huge pohutukawa trees. She could even see the red stars of their flowers, which were unusually long-lasting this year. She could see people on the main street of the village, stopping to talk to each other as they went about their tasks for the day, the pace of life here encouraging them to take their time and stop to smell the roses.

It was a view Abby adored but she'd seen it many times a day for more than five years, now. There was no excuse to be caught staring out the window during working hours. Especially right now, when she was in the middle of a heavy outpatient clinic and the island's only doctor at the moment, Ben McMahon, was out on a house call.

She'd been actively trying to persuade mothers to bring their children to this clinic for weeks, determined to make sure that every baby and preschool child on the island was up to date with their vaccinations. She had a responsibility to keep things moving as efficiently as possible because she'd hate Ben to come back and find chaos.

Ruth had her six-week-old baby, Daisy, in her arms and a very active toddler, Blake, who was trying to climb up onto the examination couch.

'You want to sit up there?' Abby scooped up the little boy and sat him on the bed. 'Don't move, okay? We'll both get into trouble if you fall off.'

Coming up to two years old, Blake was overdue for his protection against some of the more dangerous childhood viruses like measles, mumps and chickenpox. Baby Daisy was due for her polio drops as well as an injection. Right now, Blake was grinning up at Abby but he'd be crying very soon, unfortunately. It was never enjoyable having to inflict pain on small children, even if it was for the greater good. Ignoring the ping of a heartstring, Abby reminded herself that she could at least cheer the older children up pretty fast with a bright 'I've been brave' sticker and a sugar-free jelly snake.

Maybe that reluctance to inflict pain could explain the procrastination of getting caught by the view.

Except it was more than that. Abby had been the clinic's senior nurse for years now. She was experienced and professional, and personal feelings were not allowed to interfere with her job. What was bothering her so much? She couldn't help another frowning glance outside as she went to the fridge to collect the vaccines she needed.

Ruth removed her breast from Daisy's mouth and got up from her chair to have a look out the window herself, rocking baby Daisy when she started grizzling about having her feed interrupted. A moment later, she was also frowning.

'You're right,' she told Abby. 'Something doesn't feel quite right, does it?'

'You feel it, too?' Abby was holding the small glass vials in her hand, warming them up so the injections might be less painful. 'It's weird, isn't it?'

'There's nothing out there that I can see.'

'No. It's kind of like that feeling you get when you've gone on holiday and you're on the plane and then you suddenly wonder if you've left the iron on, or a tap running or something.'

Ruth laughed. 'Can't say I've ever worried about an iron. We're lucky to get enough hot water from solar power. Clothes stay wrinkly in my house.'

The laughter broke the shared unease.

'My mother used to tell me off for worrying too

much,' Abby confessed. 'She said I was a born worry-wart and I was never happy unless I had something to worry about and if there wasn't anything real, I'd just make something up.'

And that was definitely a truthful statement.

Of course she was an expert in the mental game of finding potential causes for a premonition that something bad was going to happen. She'd been doing this kind of thinking since she was three years old. Imagine a disaster, think of every possible reason for it to have happened and then take steps to make sure it *didn't* actually happen.

It was why she'd come to Kaimotu Island in the first place, wasn't it?

Why she hadn't even tried fighting to keep the man she absolutely knew would prove to be the love of her life.

'Maybe it was that earthquake a few weeks ago,' Ruth suggested. 'It was enough to get everybody a bit on edge and old Squid hasn't helped with his forecasting doom and gloom about the "big one" being so imminent. There's a few people upset at the way he chased off the last of the summer tourists.'

Abby laughed. 'And then all we get is that tiny tremor the other day that most people barely noticed. I hear that poor Squid's been getting a hard time about that being the "big one".'

Ruth grinned. 'Squid says they'll all be laughing on the other side of their faces soon enough.'

Abby shook her head. Even the larger of the two tremors had been pretty minor. Certainly not enough to make anyone take any more notice of what the island's oldest fisherman, Squid Davies, had to say about it being a warning of the kind of quake his grandfather had experienced here. It had just been a bit of a rattle. The kind anyone who'd grown up in New Zealand was familiar with.

'Jack said it was really fun at school the next day. They got to practise their "Drop, Cover and Hold" emergency drill. I think the kids all thought it was just as good as a game of sardines, squeezing in under their desks.'

She snapped off the top of an ampoule and put the needle of a tiny one-mil syringe in to suck up the contents.

'Ahh….' Ruth was nodding. *'That's* what it is.'

'What what is?'

'Why you're on edge and staring out the window so often.'

Abby raised her eyebrows. She was all set to give Daisy her shot now but she stood there for a moment, holding the kidney dish, waiting for Ruth to elaborate.

'Jack's only just started school and he's your only child. I remember what that was like, wondering if anyone else could take care of your baby as well as you could.'

'I've been working since Jack was three. He's been in day care and play groups for half his life, just about.'

'Yeah, but he's off on the big junior school trip today, isn't he? My Brooke and Amber have gone, too. The hike to the shipwreck this morning and then the visit to the old copper mines after the picnic?'

'Mmm.' Abby bit her lip. 'I would have gone as parent help but I'd already organised this clinic and I

couldn't postpone it when I was out there trying to persuade everyone to come.'

Ruth was right. Anxiety about her precious little boy
was undoubtedly the cause for her underlying sense of
unease.

Abby's sigh was part relief, part exasperation. Enough
of this.

She could hear a child crying in the waiting room
outside and had to hope people weren't getting too
impatient. It would be disappointing if some of them
changed their minds about being here after all her hard
work of talking to parents at the local schools and play-
groups recently. Ben's younger sister Hannah was in
charge of keeping them all organised and entertained
but there was only so much a seventeen-year-old could
do to manage a room full of youngsters.

Ruth was exactly the kind of result Abby had wanted
when she'd embarked on this project. Kaimotu Island,
being so isolated from the mainland, attracted people
who wanted to live an alternative lifestyle and Ruth
and her husband Damien lived with their six children
in a converted train carriage out on the edge of the
bush. They supplemented their self-sufficient lifestyle
by making pottery that they sold to the influx of visitors in the summer months.

Totally against the idea of vaccination, Ruth and
Damien had had a huge fright last year when one of
their older children had needed urgent evacuation to
a large hospital after developing complications from
measles.

Thank goodness they weren't so isolated that evacuation wasn't a viable option in emergencies. Abby had

been in the early stages of pregnancy when she'd first arrived here and potential complications for herself or her baby had been a real worry, to put it mildly. Mix some medical knowledge in with the fervent imagination of a born worrier and obsession was well within grasp.

Reassurance had come from both the impressive skills of the doctor here, Ben McMahon, and how well the clinic was set up to either cope with a serious emergency or stabilise a patient for evacuation. And it wasn't so far by small plane or helicopter. Only a couple of hours. There was usually an abundance of private aircraft available, too, in case the mainland rescue chopper was otherwise engaged.

Thanks to the stunning scenery and the facilities that some of the vineyards had developed, Kaimotu Island was becoming an increasingly sought-after venue for weddings and honeymoons.

Predictably, Daisy's eyes widened in outrage at the prick of the needle and then she erupted into ear-splitting wails. Seeing Blake's bottom lip wobbling, Abby sighed. Why hadn't she done Blake's vaccination first? Daisy wasn't old enough to put two and two together and realise that the nurse was torturing small people in here.

Ruth was offering Daisy her breast in the hope of consoling her by finishing her interrupted feed. Abby took the jar of jelly snakes and put it on the edge of her desk.

'Me?' Blake asked hopefully.

'Very soon,' Abby promised.

'No,' Blake shouted. *'Now.'*

Abby managed a smile but the tension was skyrocketing. Heading for her desk to collect Blake's file, her gaze snagged on the photo taking pride of place beside the phone.

Taken on the first day of school just a couple of months ago, Jack's proud grin lit up his little face. A cheeky grin beneath mischievous dark brown eyes and a mop of soft, black curls. Something huge and warm welled up inside Abby and she felt some of the tension evaporate. It was always so grounding to be reminded of her love for her son. The reason she'd come here had been to keep him safe and give him the best possible start in life.

It was great that he was out having a real boy's adventure today. The teachers and other parents would be looking after him. He wasn't going to wander off and drown or topple into an abandoned mine shaft. It was ridiculous to even allow the fear of such scenarios to enter her head but they'd been there ever since Jack had started to get mobile and had crawled into his first spot of bother and revealed what a handful he was going to become.

She didn't need the photograph to remind her of what hovered in the back of her mind every single day. It was more than looks. It was a whole personality.

Jack was the spitting image of his father.

The man she had loved so much.

The man she had chosen to lose.

'Did you get put on the naughty step?'

'Reckon it was worth it.' Thomas Kendrick threw a lazy grin in his colleague's direction as he headed for the comfortable armchair in the staff quarters of the mainland rescue base.

The most recent addition to the elite team of paramedics, Felicity, shook her head. 'I'd heard you were a bit of a cowboy even before I applied for the job here, you know. Yesterday was the first time I'd actually seen you do something so reckless, though.'

Tom shrugged. Okay, the job had been a bit wild. And, yes, he'd taken a fair risk climbing under the unsecured car wreck at the bottom of a cliff as it had teetered on rocks, far too close to the boiling surf, but it had been the only way to get the unconscious driver out.

'You were just as keen as I was, Fizz. You would have been the one to crawl inside if I'd let you.'

'Yeah...' Her grin was unrepentant. 'It was awesome, wasn't it? And we got her out. Alive.'

They had. But Tom had known there would be repercussions. Felicity had sustained a fairly major laceration to her arm in the process and was now stitched up and in a dressing that had to be kept dry. She was off active duty for a few days. And Tom had received a warning from an exasperated base manager.

'Look, we both know you live for the adrenaline rush, Tank. And we both know you're the best in the business. But there are limits, okay? Start taking notice of the boundaries or I'll have to take this further than a verbal warning. You nearly broke one of the crew. That's not on.'

Fair enough. It hadn't been his fault that Fizz had got injured, though. She had simply refused to do what he'd told her and stay put, off the slippery rocks, until he'd retrieved their patient. She was too young. Too eager.

And not just when it came to the job. The look she was giving him now was unambiguous.

'I'm off active duty, Tank. I'm…frustrated.'

Tom ignored the invitation in her eyes. It would be all too easy to start an affair with Felicity. The other guys on the base were probably taking bets on how long it would take this time. And they were probably getting a bit puzzled by the fact that Tom couldn't seem to summon the interest.

Maybe the game of starting something he would only want to finish not so far down the track was finally getting old. Been there, done that. Too many times.

'You could come and help me with a…a stocktake, maybe…'

Counting supplies in the storeroom was not what Felicity had in mind. Good grief…at *work*? Maybe he did push the boundaries when it came to saving lives out in the field but, dammit, he had some personal boundaries. Funny that the prospect of an illicit thrill wasn't even enough to spark real desire, though.

He shook his head. 'I'm going to hit the gym. Doubt if we'll get another job before the shift's over.'

He knew she was watching him as he left the room. He knew he could pretty much click his fingers and get her into his bed if he wanted. Was that the problem? That there was no challenge involved?

The rescue base pilot on duty, Moz, was running on the treadmill. He raised a water bottle in salute as Tom entered the small fitness centre. The paramedic standing in for Fizz was Frank and he was currently using the rowing machine.

That wasn't the name his parents had given him, of

course. It was short for Frankenstein and had been be-
stowed after an accident had given him an impressive
facial laceration. The scar from the injury was virtually invisible, now, but the nickname had well and truly
stuck.

Stripping off his overalls, Tom moved to the weight
machine, wearing only a pair of shorts and a singlet.
He flexed his muscles and started to warm up slowly.
Keeping in shape was taking more effort these days but
it was worth it. He'd earned his own nickname years ago
due to his physique, along with his impressive height.

Thomas the Tank Engine. Unstoppable.

The weights on the machine rattled loudly and Tom
narrowed his eyes as he watched them. The whole machine was rocking now and he wasn't touching anything.

'What the hell is that? An *earthquake*?'

'Didn't feel a thing.' Moz was still pounding the
treadmill at a good pace.

'I felt it.' Frank was looking interested rather than
alarmed in any way.

An earthquake you were aware of was pretty unusual
for Auckland, but not unheard of. They had minor tremors all over the country on a regular basis. If that was
it, it was nothing to write home about.

Frank was already moving to his next activity. 'Just
a seismic burp,' he said. 'No biggie.'

'Might be the tail end of something that was pretty
big for someone else,' Tom suggested.

Frank grinned. 'That would make up for a quiet day,
wouldn't it?'

Moz mopped the sweat from his brown with a hand towel but didn't slow down. 'Dream on,' he called.

Tom laughed. They would probably all do exactly that for the next few minutes. Good distraction from the pain of pushing yourself physically, anyway, imagining an event that could provide the kind of job they all dreamed of.

Tom took a deep breath and released it. He was feeling good now. Life was full of exciting possibilities. You just needed to be in the right place at the right time.

And keep yourself fit.

Tom added more weights and settled into his routine.

The tremor on Kaimotu Island started exactly the way the others had in the last few weeks. A sharp, unpleasant, jolting sensation.

But instead of fading away, this time the intensity built up with a speed too fast to process. It wasn't until she was virtually thrown off balance and only stopped herself falling by catching the edge of her desk that Abby realised that something huge was happening. She watched the jar of jelly snakes float through the air and then smash into shards on the floor. The fridge door had opened and its contents were starting to spill out. The revolving filing system, filled with thousands of patient files, was rocking violently and spewing paper in all directions.

Even then, it was all happening too fast to feel any fear. Blake had been thrown off balance but was still on top of the examination couch. Any second now, though, he would be on the floor amongst the broken glass and whatever else was about to come loose. It felt like Abby was trying to move against the deck of a violently rolling ship as she lunged towards the toddler.

'Under my desk,' she shouted at Ruth. 'Quick.'

She had to shout. It wasn't just the crashing and banging of things falling around them, there was a peculiar roaring sound. As if a huge jet was trying to land on the narrow, unsealed road that led to this hilltop hospital.

Catching Blake in her arms, Abby made a dive for her desk. She felt something crunch under her knees but was oblivious to any pain. The shock of being narrowly missed by the computer monitor crashing off the desk beside her was more than enough distraction. The fridge had not only emptied its contents on the floor but now it was trying to walk through the debris, tilting ominously as it rocked from side to side.

Was the solid wood of the desktop going to be enough to protect them if the fridge fell over? Was the building going to stay upright? Vicious sounds of windows exploding and a scream from the waiting room gave Abby another surge of adrenaline, and it was then that the first shaft of pure fear sliced through her.

'Hang on,' she told Ruth. 'It's got to stop. It'll be okay.'

Who was she trying to reassure? The terrified mother who was clutching her infant with one arm and hanging on to a leg of the desk with the other? The small boy in her own arms, who was rigid with terror?

Herself?

All of them. It felt like this was never going to stop. The floor was tilting beneath them and still things were coming off the walls and shelves above, like the framed certificates that showed the qualifications Abby had worked so hard for. Heavy medical textbooks and the plastic models of joints that she used for educational purposes. Her whole world seemed to be literally crashing down around her.

And then, finally, it began to fade. The shaking stopped. The roaring noise and the sound of things breaking stopped.

Even the sound of her own breathing stopped.

Abby had never heard a silence quite like this.

Heavy.

Dead.

The moment when the world changed irrevocably.

And that was the moment that real fear took hold. When it had all stopped but you couldn't know if it was about to start again.

Or what had happened to everybody else.

Oh, God… *Jack*…

CHAPTER TWO

THE PILOT TOOK the rescue helicopter in a long, slow sweep over the length of Kaimotu as they made their final approach.

Most of the island appeared to be covered in native bush with little in the way of buildings. Housing was concentrated along the longest stretch of beach and the hills at one end. This was where the wharf was located and the community's centre, which contained the public buildings, including schools and business premises.

It was also where the major damage from the earthquake had been focused according to the patchy reports that had been coming in for nearly two hours now. The tremor that Tom and his colleagues had felt had indeed been the tail end of something much bigger. A seven point four earthquake with its epicentre right beneath Kaimotu Island. Probably right beneath its most densely populated area at this time of day, unfortunately. Reports contained the information that there were a lot of people injured. Possibly trapped in collapsed buildings.

The landing coordinates were for the field close to the medical centre, which was often used for evacuations from the island. This was the first time Tom had ever been here but it was hard to appreciate the natural beauty of the isolated island with the amount of adrenaline he had coursing through his body. Exchanging a glance with Frank as they hovered over the centre of the tiny township, where the buildings had taken the brunt of the damage, he could see that his mate was as wired as he was.

Here they were, the first responders, quite possibly the only responders for some time, and they were facing what was probably going to be the biggest job of their careers.

'There it is.' The voice of Moz, the pilot, sounded deceptively calm. 'The medical centre. Hang on to your hats, boys. Let's get this baby on the ground.'

In their bright red overalls, still wearing their white helmets with the rescue service insignia on the front, hefting only their backpacks full of emergency gear, Tom and Frank ducked beneath the slowing rotors and ran for the steps leading up to the modern buildings attached to the old, wooden hospital. A sign indicated that this was the island's medical centre—the place they'd been instructed to report to first.

Even before they got through the door they could see the place was crowded. There were people milling around inside and out and the veranda of the old hospital was packed.

It had been two hours since the quake had struck. The initial tsunami warning had been cancelled when it had become clear that the quake hadn't been centred out at sea. Were people staying on higher ground anyway, just in case?

How many of the walking wounded had made it this far? How many had been carried here? Tom had no idea what was available in terms of medical staff and resources. He had to hope that somebody competent had taken charge and would be able to fill him in. Where would they be needed most? How on earth would they even begin to triage this situation?

The waiting room was packed to the gills. The sound of children crying and the sight of so many pale, frightened people galvanised Tom into action.

'Who's in charge here?' he asked the person closest to the door, a middle-aged woman who was holding a bloodstained dressing against long grey hair that was matted with blood.

'The nurse. A—*Ahhh...*' The word turned into a shriek of fear as the building shook. Children screamed. Somebody tried to push past Tom to get to the door. Everybody else was moving now, too. Gathering children into their arms and either crouching over them or turning to flee.

Tom turned to say something to Frank but all he could manage was a quiet but fervent oath. The aftershock was over almost as soon as it had begun but his heart was still picking up speed as he surveyed the room, wondering if the building was about to come down on them all.

'It's just an aftershock.' The clear notes of a woman's voice cut through the sounds of panic. 'We have to expect them. You're all safe in here. Mike and Don have checked the building. It's solid.'

'Who are Mike and Don?' Frank's query came as Tom tried to see past all the people and find the woman who'd spoken. There was something about that voice that had made his gut tighten instantly. Sent a tingle down the length of his spine. 'And where are they now?'

'Let's find out.' Taking a step forward, Tom found a space magically clearing, the way it usually did when they arrived on scene. They had come to help. They knew what they were doing. Their arrival was always welcome.

He could see the back of the woman now. A long blond braid hung down over a navy blue uniform. Tom felt that kick in his guts again but the sight of long blond hair always did that to him, didn't it? Ever since…ever since…

Abby…

'It's definitely broken,' he heard her tell a teenage boy as she finished winding a crepe bandage to hold a cardboard splint in place on his arm.

Now that her name was filling his head, it was easy to recognise that voice. Clear, soft notes that got a husky little edge to them when she was stressed. Or when she was…

No. Tom had to force that particular association out of his mind as fast as it had entered but it was by no means easy because there *was* a husky edge to her voice right now.

'It won't hurt so much now it's immobilised but I'm sorry, Sean—there's nothing more I can do right now. We'll all have to wait until help arrives.'

'It's here,' the boy told her, staring up at Tom, his eyes wide. 'Right behind you.'

The woman rose to her feet in a graceful movement, turning at the same time. Tom could clearly see the re-lief in her eyes as she registered the bright uniforms of the helicopter crew. And then he saw the shock as she caught his gaze.

As she recognised him.

'Oh, my God... *Tom*...?'

The shock was mutual. Tom had thought that being on an island in the aftermath of a massive earthquake was the only thing he'd be expected to have to deal with.

But he'd been so wrong.

Seeing Abby again was...was such a shock he couldn't even begin to process it.

That hair, with its gorgeous golden-honey colour and the length that made it so damn sexy when it brushed on naked skin.

Her voice...

Those huge blue eyes that darkened in colour if her mood was extreme. They were as dark as he'd ever seen them right now. She was shocked. Afraid.

Of *him*?

It was another reaction that Tom had to squash. This wasn't about them right now. It couldn't be allowed to be. And this was most certainly not the time or place to try to process anything so personal.

So Tom simply nodded. And acknowledged her.

'Abby.'

It was just a name but the weight that single word could carry was overpowering. It wasn't just a person he was acknowledging. Behind that name swirled deep, personal things. Huge, *painful* things that Tom had thought were long since dead and buried. He could feel them hovering over him in this instant, waiting to punch him in the gut with far more force than seeing her hair or hearing her voice had done. Stab him in the heart, even.

They couldn't be allowed to get even remotely closer. Not here, not now. They were in an emergency situation that was far bigger than a reunion between two people whose relationship had turned to custard.

'Fill us in,' he ordered Abby. 'Communication's been very patchy and we need to know what we're dealing with, here.'

She nodded. 'The cell phone tower is out of action. They've been using the coastguard radio to communicate with the mainland but nobody's been back to update us. We had no idea when help would start arriving. Come with me.'

Abby led them to what had been her office.

Tom Kendrick was here.

Here. Right behind her. As huge as he'd ever been in both his physical size and the sheer presence his personality emanated. Just as breathtakingly gorgeous as he'd ever been, too, with those strong features and dark eyes and that deep, commanding voice. A crisp, professional voice right now but Abby knew how it could soften. How both that voice and those eyes could make her think of melted chocolate.

Oh…dear Lord… The past was crashing all around her, just like all that stuff that had come off the shelves of her office during the big quake.

Small, paper-sized things, like finding out they had the same favourite foods. Sweet, jelly-snake kinds of things, like how good the sex had been. Huge, fridge-sized things, like the way she couldn't have imagined her future without him as a part of it.

She couldn't handle this new bombardment. Her world had been turned upside down and shaken far too hard already. Abby walked ahead of Tom, frantically trying to find the emotional equivalent of a solid desk to crawl underneath, but every instinct was urging her to run. To get out of there—away from Tom—to find Jack and then just keep running. The way she had when Jack had been no more than a positive line on a pregnancy test?

No. Her first instinct then had been to run back to Tom, hadn't it? Despite the fact that their relationship had already hit the rocks. She'd chosen to run later, when she'd had time to think about the implications of a future that included him.

Something like a sob was building inside her chest, making it impossible to take a breath. She couldn't run because she was desperately needed here.

And she didn't even know where Jack was right now, so she could find herself running totally in the wrong direction.

The hovering terror had just been magnified.

She didn't know whether Jack really was safe.

And...what if Tom found out about Jack?

She had to hold it together. She would be no use to anyone if she fell apart. She had to hang on to the mantra that Ruth had given her within minutes of the quake. Jack was safe. All the children on the school trip, including her Brooke and Amber, would be safe. They were miles away from the township and village and the falling debris that was hurting people.

They were probably the safest people on the island and the teachers would be looking after them. The only reason that they weren't already in the school hall that was being used as an evacuation centre was because something had happened to close the cliff road. They might have to walk instead of riding in the old school bus.

Time had passed in a blur since that initial terror. That first stunned silence, when the wail of the tsunami-warning siren could be clearly heard, hadn't lasted long.

Panicked people were heading away from the harbour's edge and uphill towards the hospital. Others began rushing away from the medical centre when it was discovered that the cell phone tower was obviously not functioning and there was no way for anybody to find out whether loved ones were okay. The first injured people began to arrive and Abby had to check on the mostly elderly inpatients in the old hospital wing.

She needed Ben to be here. And Ginny, the doctor who'd helped out recently, although she was refusing to fill the gap that had been left when the last doctor had resigned. She wouldn't refuse now. They needed all the help they could get.

Thank heavens for Ruth. She'd started by reassuring Abby about the children and had then carried on to be a tower of strength in assisting her to create some order amongst the chaos. With Daisy strapped to her chest in a sling, and Blake being looked after by Hannah, they'd checked on everybody they could find and dispensed both first aid and as much reassurance as they could muster. They'd been ready for contact from the local policeman and volunteer fire brigade when it came and had begun to coordinate a response.

More people who needed medical attention had begun to arrive at the centre and the men had driven off to assess the damage in the township. Now Ruth was sitting at the desk in Abby's office, trying to record and coordinate information about who was missing, injured or might need evacuation to the mainland.

Ruth looked up as Abby entered the office and she had tears of relief in her eyes as she registered the men with her. 'Oh, thank God you're here.' She tilted her head to see past the two men.

'It's just us, so far.' It was the man with Tom who spoke. 'We got dispatched as soon as it was known that the epicentre of the quake was in a populated area. When contact was made and we heard about injuries and trapped people, a full response was put into action but it takes time to scramble the right people. There's another chopper and a light plane coming that are carrying two doctors, a mobile triage unit and a USAR team with a search dog, but it'll be at least an hour until they're due to land.'

Tom was looking at Abby.

'Who's in charge of the overall incident control?'

Abby heard her breath come out in an incredulous huff.

He didn't seem to be having any trouble dealing with the fact that they were seeing each other for the first time in nearly six years. Maybe it was so far in the past he didn't have things hurtling around in his head, like the image Abby suddenly got, of being cradled in his

arms. That magic time when desire had been tempo-
rarily sated and the world had never seemed so perfect.

Maybe he didn't have things crashing around in his
head or his heart, because it had never meant that much
to him in the first place. She had to hold on, here. To
stop allowing the past to intrude and assume an impor-
tance it had no right to have. She had to focus. To respond to Tom as the person he was at this moment. A
rescuer. A skilled professional who was doing exactly
what he should be doing and focusing on his job.

But…this was an *incident*?

No. This was far more than a mere incident. Her
whole community was in danger. People she loved. A
place she loved. The sanctuary she had sought years
ago that had embraced her and kept her safe. More importantly, had kept Jack safe.

Until now.

But this was Tom all over, wasn't it? This wasn't
about the people and their broken lives. This was about
the adrenaline rush of a big job. Of the opportunity to
put himself in danger to save others.

Not her problem. Abby could hear the almost desperate
whisper in the back of her mind. Not anymore.

Tom was staring at her. Holding her gaze but keeping anything personal well shuttered. If he knew what
she was thinking—and, given what she knew about
him, he probably did—he wasn't about to let it interfere with his work.

Oh…help. For a heartbeat, Abby was caught by that
intense stare. Or rather by what she could see around it.
The gorgeous olive skin and strong features that spoke

of Maori heritage. Those dark, dark eyes. The soft, dark waves of hair.

An adult version of her precious Jack.

She couldn't go there. Couldn't waste another second thinking about what Tom looked like. Or how it made her feel, seeing him again like this.

'Mike Henley is our senior police officer. He's working with Don Johnson, who's the chief fire officer. They have about twenty people who work in the volunteer fire brigade and have had some training in rescue. We also have our island coastguard guys. They've set up headquarters in the information centre, which is on the main street at the ferry terminal end. A boat radio is being used to contact the mainland. The cell phone tower is down.'

'What medical staff are available? Where are your doctors?'

'We only have one full-time doctor on the island at the moment—Ben McMahon. He was out on a house call when the quake happened and we haven't heard any news since. There is another doctor but she's not working officially and I have no idea where she is at the moment. Apart from that, we have four nurses. Two of them are on duty in the hospital. The others are on their way and they're going to help look after injured people after we've assessed and stabilised them.'

'We?'

Abby felt a flush of colour stain her cheeks. 'So far it's only been me. Fortunately there hasn't been anything major arriving.'

'We need to get to the information centre. And we

need a medical team to work with. What's the most serious case you've got in here?'

'There's nothing life-threatening. Bruises, lacerations and a few broken bones. One of our other nurses who's coming in is trained in first aid. It's under control.'

'Good. You can come with us, then.'

It was a gasp rather than a huff that escaped Abby now. 'I don't think so.... This is where people are coming for treatment.'

'If they can get themselves here, they're not the victims we need to worry about first. We've got doctors arriving very soon and they can base themselves here. You're an experienced emergency nurse, Abby. We're going to need more than one team to check the township and triage for injuries. Frank can lead one. You can come with me. I take it you know the layout of the town?'

'Of course. I've been living here for five years.'

A flicker crossed Tom's face as he registered that this was where she'd come after they'd split up. A frown that suggested he couldn't understand why. It was gone as fast as it had appeared but Abby was aware of a flash of...what, satisfaction? *Relief?* He wasn't as unaffected as he was managing to appear. He hadn't forgotten everything because he hadn't cared enough.

Yes. It was a kind of relief. She wasn't the only one who was finding this painful.

'Good.' Tom's gaze had shifted away from her. 'You'll know the people as well, then. Could be a valuable asset.'

Torn, Abby twisted her head to look at Ruth. She

could see her own reaction reflected back. She was a valuable asset here, too, wasn't she? This felt like the right place to be. Where she had access to medical equipment and drugs and where Ben and Ginny would come to help.

This was where someone would come to reunite Jack with his mother.

And…and it was a much safer place to be than out there in the unknown, where things were wrecked and dangerous and where she could be at serious risk if there were any more of those horrible aftershocks.

But these new arrivals were the experts. They also had medical qualifications that exceeded her own. Ethically, she had no choice. She had to follow orders.

'Let's go.' Frank was staring out the window. 'We're wasting time here, mate.'

Tom's glare was holding Abby. Pulling her in.

'I can't go out like this.' Abby held out her bare arms and looked down at the flimsy material of her uniform.

'There's the overalls in the back of the Jeep,' Ruth reminded her. 'And the helmets.'

'You've got a four-wheel-drive vehicle?' Tom was moving towards the door. 'Excellent. Let's move.'

The Jeep was one of the clinic's vehicles, modified to have a stretcher clipped in the back and equipped with emergency gear. The island's equivalent of an ambulance. Ben had the other one.

'Go, Abby,' Ruth urged. 'We can cope here. People need you.'

Abby nodded. She had no choice. Tom was already halfway out the door. Frank was holding back, waiting for Abby to go ahead of him.

'Send someone to find me,' she told Ruth, 'if you hear anything at all about Jack.'

'Of course I will. He'll be fine, Abby. They all will.'

But Ruth's lips trembled. She had two daughters on that school trip, didn't she? Did she have to try and make Abby believe they were all safe in order to keep herself focused?

'Who's Jack?' Frank asked as he followed Abby out of the door. 'Your husband?'

'No.' Abby took a deep breath as she tried to push her own fear back into its box in the corner. 'He's my... my son.'

Tom heard.

Abby had a child? A *son*?

Of course she'd moved on. It had been nearly six years since they'd been together. How old was this Jack? A baby? A toddler, maybe. Couldn't be any older unless she'd moved on and replaced him pretty damn fast.

'So you've got a son?' The words escaped as Tom climbed into the front passenger seat of the Jeep.

Abby reached to switch on the ignition. 'Mmm.'

'And he's in day care or something, because you're working?'

She might have nodded. It was hard to tell because she was turning her head to see whether Frank was on board and the door was closed. It was also quite possible she was avoiding answering him by simply pretending she hadn't heard his question.

'How old is Jack?' Tom knew it was none of his business. He had no right to ask personal questions and it was entirely inappropriate given the circumstances but the idea that Abby had moved on so conclusively…had had a *child* with her new man was sitting in his gut like a hot rock right now. Burning, even.

The vehicle lurched forward with enough force to make him think about fastening his seat belt instead.

'Sorry,' Abby said. 'Haven't driven this beast for a while. It's a bit rugged.'

'No worries,' Frank said dryly. 'We just won't hand you the controls for the helicopter any time soon.'

Even when Abby was used to the clunky transmission again, the ride was no smoother. The road was badly damaged with parts that had risen into hillocks and other parts sunken and cracked. There were pools of…

'What is that?' Abby asked.

'Liquefaction,' Tom responded. 'Silt gets driven up through the earth. Don't drive into it. It may be filling a sinkhole and could be deep. We'd get stuck.'

Abby was now manoeuvring the vehicle very competently, driving onto the grass verge at times to avoid obstacles. For a moment, Tom stopped looking through the windscreen to spot hazards and looked at her face instead.

He saw a grimly determined profile. She must be scared stiff, he thought. She'd never been into the adrenaline rush of facing danger. She was the total opposite of someone like Fizz. Unlike any of the women he'd ever been attracted to or involved with—before or after Abby, in fact—and maybe *that* had been the attraction in the first place. It had also been the reason it could never have worked long-term. He needed to remind himself of that. Had to fight an undercurrent happening here that he didn't even want to try and identify.

And Abby was not only facing potential personal danger here. This was her home now and people she knew well could be amongst the dead and injured. And her child was missing? Yet here she was, totally focused on what had to be done. Heading further into danger?

Tom felt a strong impulse to send her back up the hill when he and Frank had been delivered to where they needed to go. To keep her safe.

Except they needed all the medical assistance they could get. The whereabouts of the only other medics on the island were unknown. Sure, the volunteer fire brigade or civil defence guys here would be trained in first aid but he'd seen Abby in action in an emergency department. He knew she would be as capable as he was of getting an IV line in under difficult circumstances. Assessing someone's injuries. Intubating them if necessary. She was more than capable. Abby was gifted. Working as a GP's nurse on a remote island must be sadly underutilising her skills.

If hitting another bump wasn't enough to bring his train of thought instantly back to his present surroundings, entering the main street of the village certainly was.

'Oh...my God,' Abby breathed. She slowed the vehicle, looking stunned as she took in the scene.

It must have been a very picturesque shopping centre with its old, heritage brick and stone buildings preserved and restored to enhance it as a tourist destination but they were always the type of buildings that came off worst in an earthquake. Shop facades and chimneys had toppled. Walls had crumbled, leaving skeletons of wooden framing and rooms exposed like an open doll's house.

A car was buried under a crushing mound of bricks, with only the front wheels and bumper clearly visible.

'Hope there wasn't anybody inside,' Frank said quietly.

A few metres on there was another mound of bricks and timber. There were several men here, frantically pulling at chunks of rubble. They flagged down the Jeep.

'We need help. There's someone under here.'

'Are they calling?' Tom asked.

The man shook his head, his face twisted with distress. 'We can see her foot.'

Tom took a deep breath. 'I'm sorry, mate, but there's no chance she'll be alive under there.'

'I know...' The man dragged in a ragged gulp of air. 'But we've got to try...'

'You need to keep yourselves safe.' Tom pointed upwards. 'Another aftershock could bring that lot down. Who directed you to dig here?'

He shook his head. 'We just arrived.'

'Follow us to the information centre. We're going to get a plan in place for a systematic search and rescue effort. We'll need all the help we can get.'

He turned to Abby, who was staring in horror at the gap the men were opening up in the pile of rubble. Could she see the part of the woman's body being exposed? Was it someone she knew?

He wanted to reach out. To touch her arm and offer encouragement. Strength. Or comfort, maybe. But he would be crossing a boundary to do that. The same boundary that made it inappropriate to want to send her back to the hospital to protect her. They were no longer in any kind of relationship. Quite the opposite, and Abby would not want to reach out in any way. The boundary was an almost palpable thing. Like a glass bubble encasing Abby.

'Drive on, Abby,' Tom said quietly. 'We can't stop.'

This was far, far worse than Abby had anticipated, but it felt so unreal she knew she wasn't going to fall apart. It was like being transported onto the set of a disaster movie and she was merely a character waiting to play her part depending on the instructions of the director.

Feeling as though she was on autopilot, she kept the vehicle going until they reached the other end of the main street. The wharf end, where the ferries berthed. She could see a police car among all the vehicles parked outside the information centre, a modern hexagonal structure that was central enough to make it an excellent choice as an operational hub.

The men who were currently the directors looked as though they were up against it.

The island had three police officers and Mike Henley was the most senior. The biggest 'incident', as Tom would call it, that Mike had had to deal with in recent years had been a private yacht that had gone aground in rough weather on Elephant Rocks, which were far enough offshore to have made the rescue fairly dramatic.

Mike's best mate was Don Johnson, who was the chief fire officer for Kaimotu Island. He was also in charge of civil defence and the coastguard and, in fact, he'd been the one who'd dealt with the Elephant Rocks incident very competently.

Both men had come past the hospital on the way into the town's centre as soon as this emergency had struck and they'd taken the time to check, as best they could, that the building that would be required for providing medical aid was safe to be inside. When the two men saw Abby come into the information centre with Tom and Frank, their relief was obvious. Expert help had started to arrive, at last.

And Abby was proud to introduce him to Tom. If anyone had asked her who she would want to turn up if she was ever in a dangerous situation and needed her life saved, Tom Kendrick would be at the very top of her list.

Even after they'd broken up.

Maybe even more so, because she knew that Tom still wouldn't hesitate to do whatever it took to save her, even if it meant he was putting his own life at risk. And it wasn't because he was stupid and a cowboy, as some had accused him of being. Or that he had some kind of death wish. He could calculate those risks perfectly well. He was just prepared to push the boundaries further than most.

Abby was a born worrier. She could conjure up imaginary disasters with no effort whatsoever. The habit was as ingrained as the way she tied shoelaces or slept with her head cradled in the crook of her elbow.

What would Tom think if he knew about some of the fantasy situations she'd come up with over the years? The ones that always ended with his appearance to make everything okay? The ones where he saved her and held her in his arms afterwards as if she was the most precious thing on earth? Or the ones where he saved Jack and recognised his own son?

Oh…help…

This was no fantasy. Abby stood quietly to one side as the group of men taking control of this rescue operation made swift plans. The wall behind them was covered with the kind of brochures the tourists were looking for the moment they arrived on Kaimotu Island. Invitations to charter a fishing vessel or go scuba diving. Pictures of people happily abseiling, mountain biking or taking a vineyard tour. The kind of activities Kaimotu was famous for and which now seemed no more than fantasies themselves.

A map of the township was on a table and grids had been drawn on it. There were cans of spray paint in a box on the floor. They were going to be assigned areas and would spray information on the walls about what they found. Whether there were people trapped. Or needing urgent attention for their injuries. Or dead. If they came across serious injuries, they could only take the time for an initial stabilisation and then summon backup for transportation to the hospital. They had to keep moving as fast as possible.

There was no way Tom's presence was going to be enough to make everything okay here, either. It was going to take a lot of people and a lot of time. They were facing a gruelling night of probably grim and possibly dangerous work.

There was also absolutely no chance of Tom taking her in his arms and holding her, and that was a good thing. She was over him. She'd spent years getting over him and she couldn't afford to let those protective walls around that place in her heart fall apart.

And surely there was no chance that Tom would instantly see himself in Jack, was there? She'd managed to avoid letting Tom know exactly how old Jack was, which would be a dead giveaway, and there shouldn't be any need for the two of them to be in the same place at the same time.

When Jack and the other children turned up, they would be cared for in the community centre. She would be able to get there and reassure herself that he was fine and then she could have him go to Ben's parents, Doug and Ailsa. Or Hannah, up at the hospital.

Somehow she had to keep Jack hidden from Tom.

At least until she had some time to try and think this through.

Abby barely heard the last instructions being issued by Tom and Mike and Don. She tightened the straps on her backpack full of medical supplies.

'So you'll be Tom's partner,' Mike said, as though summarising everything she hadn't heard clearly enough. 'You're going to triage the northern half of the village but if we need you for major medical stuff, you'll be contacted by radio.'

Abby could only nod.

Tom's *partner*.

How ironic was that?

At least they had an urgent mission to focus on. No time for anything personal to interfere with the job that needed to be done.

No time to herself to try and think things through.

To try and deal with the awful dread that she had, in fact, done a terrible thing by not making more of an effort to tell Tom about Jack a long time ago.

CHAPTER THREE

THE CHOPPING BEAT of a hovering helicopter was loud enough to preclude the need for any conversation as Tom and Abby stepped out of the information centre, which had now morphed into the island's incident control headquarters.

Abby was shading her eyes against the lowering sun to peer upwards.

Tom raised his voice, although the chopper was moving again, now. 'That'll be the extra doctors arriving. And maybe the first USAR team members. Hopefully with a search dog.'

He saw Abby close her eyes for a moment and take a deep breath, as though summoning a fresh burst of courage. He had to fight the urge to touch her. To offer her some of *his* strength.

'Who else will come, do you think?'

Tom didn't have to raise his voice any longer. 'I imagine the army will be involved by now. If they've got an Iroquois helicopter available they can dispatch a few troops, which will be useful. It would be good to have more space available for evacuating any serious trauma, too.' He glanced down at the map in his hand. 'Let's get going. Where's Hickory Lane? That's the southern border for our search area.'

'A few blocks up this way.' Abby set off. 'It's got a bakery on one side called The Breadbin and the Fat Duck café on the other side. There's a big metal duck sculpture that hangs off the side of the café. You can't miss it.'

Except the quirky café icon was no longer hanging off the brick wall. It was buried somewhere beneath the rubble. There were several local men standing in the middle of Hickory Lane, where it branched off the main street.

'Hey, Abby,' one of them called. 'You okay?'

'That's Jim,' Abby told Tom. 'He's our butcher. His shop's a bit further down.'

She stepped closer to the men. 'I'm fine, Jim. What about you? Oh, help…look at your hands.'

The middle-aged butcher was still wearing his blue-and-white-striped apron but it was filthy. His arms were just as grimy but they were also scratched and bruised-looking. His hands were a mess, his knuckles ripped and bleeding.

Tom saw them cupped in Abby's much smaller hands. He saw the expression on Abby's face. This man wasn't just the local butcher. He was someone Abby cared about. Part of a community she cared about. A place and a way of life that made *him* an outsider.

He didn't like that feeling.

'It's nothing.' Jim dismissed Abby's concern but his smile was grateful. 'I've just been shifting a few bricks.'

'A few!' One of the other men gave Jim a friendly thump on his shoulder. 'This man's been a right hero.

Single-handedly dug at least three people out from under where they got buried here.' He pointed at the Fat Duck.

'Everybody inside got out in time,' Jim told them. 'But poor Miriam got hit in the head by a brick or something. And some others got under the picnic table. They got buried good and proper.'

'Where's this Miriam?' Tom asked.

'We just sent her up to the hospital. Used the back of Johnno's ute. She should be there by now.'

'And the others?'

'Not too bad. We sent them all off to get checked, though.'

'So the café's clear of people?' Tom had his can of spray paint ready. 'Are you sure about that?'

Jim nodded. 'Business was pretty quiet. Miriam was last out. She was making sure all her customers were safe first, bless her.'

'Right.' Tom sprayed the word 'Clear' and the time on a window that was still intact. He could see inside the café. There were tables with plates of uneaten food on them. Toppled chairs and an abandoned handbag that was spilling its contents into the puddle created by an overturned water cooler. They needed to move on.

'Let's go, Abby. Next building. We'll do the rest of Hickory Lane and then come back to the main street.'

'What can we do to help?' Jim asked.

'Best thing you can do is head for the information centre. They'll be organising teams and giving out some safety gear and radios and things. We don't want you just off on your own. It's too dangerous.'

'I don't think there's anybody up Hickory Lane,' another of the men said. 'My wife and kids were along there and they got out fast. Everyone panicked and ran when they heard the siren go off. Someone said they should all go to the community centre in the new school hall.'

'We'll check anyway,' Tom said. 'But thanks.'

They moved swiftly along the narrow lane, climbing over rubble to peer into buildings. Yelling as loudly as they could.

'Is anyone here? Can you hear me?'

There could be people buried or too injured to respond but they would be found later by the urban search and rescue teams and the dogs in a second sweep. Right now, the priority was to try and get an idea of the big picture and find anything urgent that could be dealt with fast.

Back on the main street they came across another knot of people, these ones in front of the hardware store. They spotted the overalls and helmets Tom and Abby were wearing and backed out to make room amongst the rubble.

'We can hear someone,' a man said, clearly distressed. 'Groaning.'

Sheets of corrugated iron from the veranda roof along with timber beams were making it impossible to get any further. As they stood there, something rolled from higher up, bounced and narrowly missed Abby as it fell with a crash.

Tom gripped Abby's elbow and hauled her back. 'Everybody move back,' he ordered. 'We're going to have specialist teams here very soon.' He marked a sheet of iron beside where the men had been working. 'Trapped 1', he painted. '1725 hours'. He added an arrow pointing to the interior of the shop.

As if to back up his words to the locals, a group wearing the bright orange overalls of a USAR team appeared on the main street, walking down from where the last helicopter had landed beside the hospital. One of them had a dog, which was straining at its leash.

'Where's the info centre?' one of them called.

'Keep going that way,' Tom directed, pointing. 'And take these guys with you. We need to clear this zone of civilians.'

He and Abby moved on. The next building they checked was a book-and-toy shop. Nobody answered their calls and he was about to declare it clear when he heard a cry from Abby. She climbed over a shelf teetering on a pile of dislodged books and headed deeper into the shop.

'Abby, stop! We don't know if it's safe.'

'It's Millie,' Abby shouted. 'Tom…come here, *quick…*'

The shop had been created inside an old cottage. A brick chimney had collapsed and brought down part of a heavy slate roof. Trapped beneath a beam of wood and a shower of bricks was a woman who looked to be in her eighties.

The heavy beam was directly over the woman's chest, weighted down at one end by most of the chimney bricks.

Abby was bent over the woman's head, desperately searching for signs of life. Breathing. A pulse. Tom could see that she wasn't going to find any. He crouched beside her.

'It's too late,' he said firmly. 'I'm sorry, Abby, but we have to keep moving.'

'But it's *Millie*…' Abby was crying. 'She's known every child on the island for generations, now. She has a story circle every Saturday morning when she reads to them. Everybody loves Millie. She…she just helped Jack choose his backpack and pencils for school…'

Tom froze. 'What did you just say, Abby?'

'That everybody loves Millie. We can't just leave her here like this.'

'About Jack.' Yes, it was a tragedy that an old lady every child on this island loved had been killed, but Tom couldn't give it any head space whatsoever. Something huge was exploding inside him. 'He's at *school*?'

Abby scrubbed tears from her face, making huge streaks amid the dust and grime already covering her skin. She gulped in air, trying to get herself under control, but she was nodding. 'He started a few weeks ago. He's on his first school outing today and I still don't know if…'

As if a switch had been thrown, Abby suddenly stopped crying. She went very, very still.

It was happening for her as well, Tom realised.

The world had stopped spinning because it needed to adjust the tilt of its axis. That 'something huge' still splintering inside Tom meant that his world would never turn in quite the same way again.

Slowly, Abby raised her gaze from Millie to Tom. Her eyes looked enormous and her face, beneath the grime, was as white as a sheet.

'Oh…*God*…' she whispered.

* * *

She had no one to blame for this but herself.

Abby had just walked off the edge of the precipice without even looking. She'd told Tom *exactly* how old Jack was. Five years and a few weeks. Given this man's intelligence, it would probably only take him two seconds to do the maths. To work out that nine months before Jack was born had been when they had been utterly in love. Unable to keep their hands off each other. Not always as careful as they could have been about protection because they had been blinded by how strongly they had felt about each other.

As blind as she had just been, stepping—no, *throwing*—herself off anything remotely resembling safe ground. But finding Millie dead had been the last straw, hadn't it, on top of the terror of the earthquake and the dreadful anxiety about Jack's whereabouts and safety.

The shock of seeing Tom again and the relentless punches of seeing the worst of the damage as their search progressed. Knowing with more and more clarity just how big a disaster her community and home had suffered.

She'd snapped. Somehow it had all coalesced into grief for a pillar of her small community and her own connection with this sweet old lady. Her son's connection.

Tom was rising from where he'd been crouched beside her. In slow motion, as if he was trying to counter the effects of being shot with a stun gun. And when he was on his feet, he stood as still as a stone. His lips barely moved as he spoke.

'Who's Jack's father, Abby?'

She couldn't say anything. Couldn't move. Couldn't even breathe.

He knew. Of course he knew. He just needed to hear her say the words. The way people did when someone they loved had just died. It wasn't real until you heard the words.

'It's me, isn't it?'

She still couldn't make her lips move. Or take enough of a breath to push it out and make words.

A glance up showed a muscle twitching on Tom's jaw. He was processing this. He was shocked, of course, but he was also…furious?

Yes. When he spoke, his voice was dangerously controlled. Almost too quiet to hear.

'And you didn't think to tell me?'

Now Abby could move. She pushed herself to her feet.

'I tried to.'

A snort escaped Tom. 'Funny…I don't remember that.'

'You weren't there. You…were off on a mission.'

It had been the final straw on that occasion. Confirmation of why their relationship could never have worked. Why it could have ruined more than one life if Abby had gone through with her intention to tell Tom he was going to be a father.

'Oh…so you couldn't have waited an hour or so?'

'I… You… It was after we'd broken up, Tom.'

He turned a glare on Abby that made her flinch. 'And that makes it okay? To *pretend* that you were going to tell me? Or maybe you did turn up at the base. After you saw the chopper take off, perhaps? When you knew I wouldn't be there?'

That wasn't fair. Abby opened her mouth to snap that he could go back and check the visitors' sign-in log if he thought she was lying but she didn't get a chance to speak. There was an ominous rumble and the ground began to shake with the biggest aftershock yet.

Abby started to turn her head to look for something to shelter under but felt herself being grabbed before she had time to think, let alone spot something. Her feet left the floor and, even as things rattled and more bricks came in through the damaged roof, Tom was moving at speed.

The aftershock had stopped by the time he reached the street but he didn't let go of Abby. He let her put her feet on the ground but kept her pinned with one arm, looking around and up as he assessed their safety, pulling her out of range of anything that could come loose and fall from roof level.

A four-wheel-drive vehicle was coming up the street. Mike Henley was driving.

'You guys all right?'

A burst of something like hysterical laughter almost escaped Abby. All right? Millie was lying dead in the shop they'd just escaped from. She could have just been killed herself. She was terrified. She didn't know where her son was or if he was all right. Tom had just learned that he was a father. Jack was *their* son.

No. It was inconceivable that either of them were 'all right' at this moment.

'I'm on my way to check the airstrip after that aftershock. There's an Iroquois on the way in. They've got army troops on board and a couple of structural engineers who can assess buildings properly. Oh, and, Abby?'

'Yes?'

'The crew of a fishing boat spotted the school bus. It's trapped on the cliff road between a couple of big slips. They've seen a bunch of kids and adults waving at them so we can assume everyone's okay. Including your Jack.'

'Oh...oh...' Abby's legs were threatening to give way. She was shaking all over and suddenly Tom's arm holding her up was very, very welcome. 'Oh, thank God...'

'Doesn't look like there's any way to clear the slips and get them out tonight but they're talking about using a chopper to drop some food and blankets to get them through the night. Right... Gotta go.' Mike gunned the engine. 'You two should stop for a break soon. There's a lot of teams ready to take over.'

One of those teams was just down the street, in fact. In front of the hardware store where Tom had left the painted message about someone being trapped. They weren't trapped any longer. A man's body, strapped to a back board, was being carefully lifted over the mangled iron and other debris.

Tom and Abby hadn't even scratched the surface of the conversation they needed to have but they weren't going to get a chance to continue it right now, either. Tom's radio crackled into life.

'Medic needed. Outside the hardware store on main street. Man having trouble breathing.'

Another voice came on that sounded like Frank. 'I'm five minutes away.'

Tom keyed the button on the radio. 'We're on to it.' He'd let Abby go to reach for his radio but it wasn't a problem. Her legs were steady now.

Jack was safe. He wouldn't even see anything terrible because, by the time the slips were cleared and the children rescued, any bodies or badly injured people would be out of public view. There was nothing Abby could do to speed up his rescue so she could direct all her energy to helping Tom. And with the fear about Jack vanquished, she was aware of a new burst of energy, which was just as well seeing as she had to trot to keep up with him.

He wasn't looking at her and seemed to be occupied in getting his backpack off without slowing down the pace. Was he still furious with her? Of course he was, but having a medical emergency to deal with meant that they wouldn't be having any personal conversations any time soon.

The longer it took the better, as far as Abby was concerned. It was a conversation to be dreaded, that was for sure. Except, curiously, she was aware of a trickle of relief that the truth was out. The burden of guilt had been there from the moment she'd left the rescue base that day without having spoken to Tom, and it had grown, bit by bit, over the years. Grown faster in the last few weeks since Jack had started school because most of the other children had dads and he was starting to ask some pointed questions about why he didn't.

Awareness of any personal sense of relief evaporated

as they reached the USAR crew, who had rescued the trapped victim from the hardware store.

'You know him?' Tom asked Abby.

'Of course. It's Harley. Owner of the shop.' Abby crouched beside the man and touched his shoulder. 'Harley? Can you hear me?'

Harley's eyes opened. So did his mouth and he tried to speak but he was struggling to breathe. Beside her, Tom was fitting the earpieces of his stethoscope but still looking up.

'What the story?' he asked.

'Chest and leg injuries, from what we could see. He was under the counter but a steel beam had come down on top of that. Took a bit of digging out and his breathing seemed to get worse pretty fast after we pulled him out.'

Tom used the shears he carried clipped to his belt to cut clear what remained of Harley's thick shirt. He listened to his chest for only moments. 'Find the chest drain kit, would you, Abby? He's got a tension pneumothorax.'

The chest injuries were allowing air to get into the wrong places, compressing Harley's lungs. It could stop his heart functioning if they couldn't relieve the pressure. Abby opened what she recognised as the airway roll in Tom's pack and found the wide-bore needle she knew he would need. By the time he had a pair of gloves on, she had an alcohol wipe opened and ready for him to grab, as well as the three-way stopcock and tape that would be needed to complete the procedure.

'Thanks.' Counting down the rib spaces, Tom cleaned the area the needle would penetrate. 'Can you check his leg injury and get a blood pressure while I do this?'

Abby used the shears to cut Harley's trousers. 'Femoral fracture,' she reported.

'I don't carry a traction splint.'

'It's not mid-shaft.'

'Okay. How 'bout starting an IV so we can get some pain relief on board?'

'Sure.'

They were working in far from ideal circumstances with their patient on a plastic board in the rubble of his collapsed shop. Their resources were also limited and people around them were in a hurry to move on, so there was unspoken pressure, yet to Abby it felt as if she and Tom were working together as a smooth team. She reached around him to get what she needed from the pack and paused in what she was doing to comfort Harley when he groaned loudly.

Tom had punctured the space between Harley's ribs and advanced the cannula far enough to release the pressure of the air filling his chest cavity. Almost immediately his breathing improved. Abby had the tourniquet on his arm and slid a cannula into place as Tom attached the three-way stopcock to the chest cannula and taped it into position. He might be busy with his own task but he wasn't missing anything Abby was doing.

'Nice work,' he murmured, as Abby flushed the IV access now established in Harley's arm. 'Could you draw up some morphine?'

Of course she could. The praise was remarkably sweet and with Harley now in no immediate danger thanks to their intervention, she could feel proud of

what she and Tom had just achieved by working together. She'd only ever done this kind of work in the
safe environment of an emergency department. Was this
what his job was like every day? Stressful procedures
under trying conditions to save lives?

As soon as Harley was stable, arrangements were
made to move him up to the hospital.

'He should probably get a proper chest drain inserted
before they fly him out,' Tom said. 'Either that or keep
to a low altitude.'

The light was starting to fade noticeably by the time
Harley was being taken away.

'Take a break,' one of the USAR team advised.
'You're not needed urgently right now and none of us
know how long the night's going to be.'

'When did you last eat?' Tom asked Abby.

'I skipped lunch,' she admitted. 'I was a bit nervous
about the big clinic I had on for this afternoon. And I
didn't eat much breakfast because I was a bit on edge
about…about…'

'Jack's first school outing?'

'Mmm.'

Tom said nothing more. Instead, he steered Abby
away from the hardware shop. Away from the street,
even, towards a small grassed area near the Fat Duck
that had a child's play area and a bench seat for super-
vising adults. He sat down and Abby had no choice
other than to sit down beside him and eat the muesli
bar he produced from a pocket.

'Hardly ideal,' Tom said wryly. 'And I probably
shouldn't be taking the time for personal issues but if

we're on a break, I can't see the harm. And I really do want to know. I think you owe me that much, Abby.'

Abby's heart thumped. Was he going to suggest she was lying again? About Jack's paternity, perhaps? That would hurt. Badly.

'Know what, exactly?'

'Why you didn't tell me.'

They were sitting side by side. Close enough to touch but there was a gap between them. Abby stared straight ahead of her, her gaze fixed, unseeing, on the child's slide. Where they were, and the emergency situation they were in the middle of, seemed to fade into the background. Abby mentally stepped back in time. To another situation that had been just as tense in its own way.

'I did intend to,' she said quietly. 'I went to the hospital but they said you'd discharged yourself. Against doctor's orders. They said you'd be at home, that it would be a couple of weeks before you were signed off as fit to fly, so I went to your apartment. When I found nobody was home, I decided you'd be hanging out at the base. Not the ideal place to break news like that but you hadn't returned any of my calls.'

She heard Tom's breath escape in an angry kind of hiss. 'You never left any messages.'

'Well...now you know why.'

'No.' The word was clipped. 'I can't say I do.'

Abby had to turn and look at him, then, because she didn't understand. She encountered a dark and determined gaze. Tom was still angry. He wanted answers. And he deserved the truth, didn't he? He was right. She owed him that much. A lot more, probably, because... he'd given her Jack, hadn't he?

'I don't know why you didn't wait. Why you didn't make any more of an effort to tell me.'

'It was because you were off on a mission,' Abby said. 'When your doctors must have told you it wasn't a good idea after you'd had a punctured lung. It was then I knew I...I just *couldn't* tell you.'

Abby had to bite her bottom lip hard to stop tears coming. Good grief, she seemed to be crying at the drop of a hat today. Emotional overload. How unfair was it to have so many huge things in her life crashing around her at the same time? She had no idea whether her little house was still standing or when she would get to cuddle Jack again. Seeing Tom after all these years would have been quite enough of a shock all by itself.

Cuddling Jack... Oh, Lord... The relief of hearing that he was safe was wearing off now. Abby was desperate to take her son into her arms and hold him tightly. So tightly he could never wriggle free and get into danger ever again.

Yet again she had to fight back tears. The physical activity on top of the totally shocking emotional rollercoaster she was on was taking its toll. Abby felt too exhausted to take any notice of the alarms ringing in her head as she crossed barriers that had been there for a very, very long time.

'I never told you much about my childhood, did I?'

'I know you lost your parents early and that you were brought up by your grandparents in a little country town.' Tom turned his head to survey what had been Kaimotu village. Was he thinking that she'd come to a place like this because it had reminded her of where she'd been raised?

He was closer to the truth than he realised.

'My parents were both mountaineers,' she told him. 'Famous for their achievements. They once did seven of the world's hardest climbs in a seven-month period. They wrote a book about it.... *Lucky Number Seven.*'

'And that's how they died? In a mountaineering accident?'

'Yep. They both got swept away by an avalanche. Their bodies were never recovered.'

'God, that's awful. How old were you?'

'Nine.'

Tom was looking at her. She could see the sympathy but she could also see a question mark. What did this have to do with her not telling him he was going to be a father?

'I was really proud of Mum and Dad,' Abby went on. 'I absolutely adored them but as I got older I began to understand how dangerous their passion was. I'd beg them not to go. And when they did, which was at least once a year, I'd stay with Gran and worry myself sick that something bad was going to happen.' Her voice wobbled and began to fade. 'That they'd never come back...'

It seemed perfectly natural that Tom take hold of her hand and hold it. Squeeze it, even.

'But...' He stopped himself after the single word, but it was enough for Abby to realise he still didn't get it.

'You were off on a mission, Tom. You lived for the danger of your job—just like my parents lived for the danger of the mountains. You obviously still do. When I found out you'd gone out on a job that day, I suddenly realised what it would be like if I told you that

I was pregnant. If you decided that you wanted to try and make things work, maybe. That you might want to be a father.'

She could feel the shock wave through her hand just before Tom released it abruptly.

'*Might* want to be a father? What the hell is that supposed to mean? That I wouldn't be prepared to take the responsibility? That I wasn't capable of stepping up to the mark?'

'No. It wasn't like that. It was—'

'What made you so damn sure I would have been a bad father?'

'*No.*' The word was even more vehement this time. Torn out of Abby. 'The opposite of that. You would have been a great father. The best. Just like you were in everything you did.'

The best paramedic.

The best lover…

She had to make him understand somehow, because Abby knew this would be very, very important for trying to move forward from this. For all of them. She sucked in a deep breath as she felt Tom's stunned silence as he processed her words. And suddenly—surprisingly—she felt calm.

'Jack would have had a hero for a dad,' she continued quietly. 'Someone a little boy would grow up worshipping. And at some point he'd start to understand how dangerous that job was. He'd start getting scared.'

Tom was absolutely silent beside her. Abby was looking straight ahead again and she had the impression that Tom was doing exactly the same thing. That it was too hard for him to look at her as she spoke. She wasn't finished yet, either. She had to keep going. Make him *really* understand.

'He'd start to realise that all those unknown people who were sick or hurt were somehow more important than *he* was. That every time his dad answered the call to go to one of them, there was a chance that he'd never come back.'

Abby had to scrub at her face and sniff loudly. Where were these tears coming from?

'I know what it's like to live with that fear,' she added brokenly. 'I didn't want it for my child. It was right then, when I found you'd gone off on a new mission when you hadn't even recovered from getting hurt in the last one, that I knew I had to find somewhere my baby would be safe. And keep him safe for as long as I possibly could because...'

Because that baby had been a part of herself.

A part of Tom.

The man she loved with all her heart and soul.

It was on the tip of her tongue to let that spill out, too, but Abby stopped herself just in time. Tom didn't need to know that. The consequences of him finding out he was a father were enough of a worry. She didn't need to make it worse by making herself vulnerable as a woman as well as a mother.

'Just because...' she finished lamely.

Tom was still sitting there silently. Maybe he would have said something but the air around them was filled with the distinctive heavy sound of an approaching Iroquois helicopter.

The hard-core rescue personnel were going to arrive in droves now and the operation to save and protect the community of Kaimotu Island would move into a new, intense phase. They couldn't stay sitting here in a quiet corner, ignoring what was really important right now.

And the four-wheel-drive vehicle that Mike had taken away to check the condition of the runway was coming back down the hill. At some speed, given the appalling condition the road was now in.

He slammed on the brakes when he spotted Abby and Tom sitting on the bench.

'Thought you'd be back at HQ,' he said. 'You won't have heard.'

Abby's heart skipped a beat. Was this going to be news about Jack?

'They're getting a food parcel together. It's your pilot who's going to do the drop, Tom. Moz? He's asking where you are.'

'What?' Tom reached for the radio clipped to his overalls and then swore softly. 'How the hell did I miss dropping that?'

'It's probably back at the hardware shop where we were working on Harley,' Abby said. 'Do we need to go and look for it?'

'No.' Mike shook his head. 'Jump in and come with me. We're running out of time because they don't want to do it after dark. You could go, too, if you like, Abby. You might get to wave at Jack, at least.'

If she liked?

Was he *kidding*? Abby jumped to her feet. Tom already had the door of the vehicle open for her to climb in.

He had an odd expression on his face.

Because he might get to wave at Jack, too? See his *son* for the first time?

Abby's hand was shaking as she reached to slam the door shut. As unbelievable as this day already was, the tension had just increased by several huge notches.

CHAPTER FOUR

THE INFORMATION CENTRE was a hive of activity as Abby and Tom arrived back in the gathering dusk.

Outside, portable generators were powering spotlights that illuminated vehicles being stocked with various supplies and people moving both towards and away from the operational hub.

Inside, the space was far more crowded and noisy than the last time Abby had been in there.

When she'd been delegated as Tom's partner. Before he'd had any idea of the real partnership they still had. One that would change the shape of the future for both of them.

The partnership of being parents...

Not that Abby could give any head space to a future that wasn't immediate. Even the excitement of possibly seeing Jack very soon was being pushed aside in the face of this controlled chaos.

How many choppers had landed on the island in the last couple of hours when she'd been working in what remained of the island's village? Or had a ferry arrived? The centre was crowded with strangers wearing the overalls and hard hats that were the uniform of people who knew how to handle an urban disaster.

One of them was wearing a fluorescent vest that had the insignia 'Incident Commander' on its back. Tom headed straight for the man but Abby had stopped in her tracks, overwhelmed by the noise and activity.

There were locals in here, too. Mike Henley was looking exhausted as he was being interviewed by a television crew and reporters.

'Yes. In hindsight, I suppose we could say that the minor tremors recently were foreshocks, but nobody can predict a major earthquake. I'm sorry, but you'll have to ask an expert those kinds of questions. We have more important things to deal with at the moment.'

'How many confirmed deaths have been reported so far, sir?'

'Three.' The grim lines on the senior police officer's face deepened.

'Can you release any names?'

'Not yet. Not until the victims have been identified and their next of kin notified.'

Other people were bustling past the obstruction the knot of media personnel were making. Someone had an armload of blankets.

'Put them in the ute outside, Kev,' someone else called. 'Who's got the food parcels?'

'Report of person trapped.' A young man waved a radio above his head. 'Building down and the dog handler reckons they've got someone alive in there.'

The reporters' attention swerved instantly away from Mike. The incident commander turned away from his conversation with Tom.

'Blue team? Over here.'

There was a surge of movement as a group of rescuers responded to the summons.

Abby still hadn't moved. Her body was aching, she realised. Especially her knee. She'd banged it on something, way back, but had no idea when. There were too many things happening around her and her head was spinning.

The relief of knowing Jack was safe was disappearing beneath fear again. She wouldn't really believe it until she could hold her son in her own arms. And what about all the other people she cared about so much on the island? Like Ben McMahon, who'd been her colleague and friend for so many years now. Where was he? He should have turned up hours ago, as soon as the disaster had happened. Or maybe he had. He could be up at the hospital right now, operating on a badly injured islander, perhaps.

Somebody here must know about Ben. And his parents, Doug and Ailsa, who, ever since she'd arrived here pregnant and vulnerable, had been like the parents Abby had never really had. Catching her breath, Abby looked around. She didn't even know how people had fared in their houses. If houses were still standing.

The smell of hot food caught her nose. In the corner of the information centre a table had been set up to dispense food and hot drinks to the rescue workers. Abby recognised the older woman who was clearly in charge. Daphne Hayward—the kind of pillar of a small community who was always in exactly the place she was most needed, usually with her sister, Flora, by her side. The 'Hayward girls', as they were known locally, always knew what was happening.

Finally, Abby could move.

'Daphne...do you know anything about Ben? He went out on a house call and didn't get back before the quake hit. I haven't heard anything...'

'Sorry, love. I haven't heard about Ben, either. Ailsa said she's sure he'll be fine. He'll be busy helping someone or other.... The phones aren't working.' Daphne's face creased in sympathy. 'You must be so worried about your little Jack but isn't it good news about the bus being spotted?'

'Mmm.' Abby choked back a sob. 'We're going out there...with food parcels...' She turned her head, trying to see where Tom was.

He was coming towards her through the crowd and his gaze caught hers. It felt like a solid connection. A path he was travelling to get to her side.

And it felt wonderful. The confusion—even the exhaustion—Abby had been aware of since coming into the centre was suddenly gone. Tom would be by her side any second now and then they would go and do whatever had to be done. Together. And she could cope, because she'd have Tom beside her.

Daphne was prattling on, telling her as much news as she could in a short space of time. Trying to offer her a cup of tea, as well, but Abby was moving again now. With Tom.

Heading for the door and the vehicle that would take them to the helicopter.

But she came to another sudden stop right outside the door of the information centre because there was a new crowd of people blocking the entrance. People she knew.

Ben...and Ginny...and Daphne's sister, Flora, and

a whole bunch of children. But it was Ben that Abby couldn't take her eyes off.

'Ben—oh, thank God you're okay. I've been so worried. Where have you been? We've been going out of our minds. Your mum—'

'She's okay?'

Oh, help… She could see the fear in his eyes. Ben didn't know that his family were safe. Wherever he'd been, he obviously had no idea what was happening in the township. Or up at the hospital. She had to reassure him.

'She's fine. As far as I know, all your family is okay. Doug's out with the searchers. Your house is intact and your mum and Hannah have set it up as a crèche. Oh…'

Another look at the children Ben had collected and the mention of the McMahon house being used as a crèche had reminded her of how much this family had done for her when she'd first arrived. When Jack had been a baby.

Jack…

'Can you clear the entrance, please?' A soldier was waving at them. Abby glared at him and didn't move.

'Why aren't you at the hospital?' Ben asked. He had Ginny's little girl, Button, in his arms now.

Abby hurriedly tried to reassure Ben that things were under control. That there were people who knew what they were doing in charge at the hospital. That she'd been out on the front line where things were really bad. She could feel her fear rising again as she spoke.

She could feel Tom moving closer behind her and she had to introduce him to Ben.

'This is Tom Kendrick…. I…we know each other.'

Abby had to bite her lip. Would it be obvious to Ben that Tom was a grown-up version of Jack? Or maybe Ginny would see it because she hadn't watched Jack growing up and she was seeing everything on the island with fresh eyes because she'd only returned recently.

No. Surely it wouldn't occur to either of them. They all had far too much to deal with and it had nothing to do with Jack's possible paternity.

'He's search and rescue from the mainland. We've been out. They wanted a nurse who knew people. I…I…'

Tom was even closer to her now. Abby could feel his arm go around her waist. Good grief…if it hadn't occurred to Ben to wonder about just how well they'd known each other in the past, this would be a dead give-away. And how hard would it be to put two and two together after that? She wasn't ready for other people to know about Tom being Jack's father so, despite longing for that contact and the reassurance it could convey, Abby moved swiftly away from the touch.

'I'm…I'm fine,' she said.

Ginny was staring at her. 'Abby, where's Jack?'

'On…on the bus.' And it was getting darker by the minute. They really had to get moving but Ben and Ginny needed to get brought up to speed, didn't they? Her mind a swirl of anxiety now, her voice faded to almost a whisper. 'We've just come back to get the chopper. They've organised a drop of blankets and food.'

What if they couldn't take off in time? Or if the teachers decided to walk everybody out along the cliff road? To climb over the obstacle of the slip? In the dark, with those rocks and the crashing surf so far below…?

'What the...?' Ben stopped speaking. He was staring at Abby now, too. Or had his gaze caught the fact that Tom's arm had come around her waist again and that, this time, she hadn't moved out of range.

'It's okay,' Tom was saying calmly, over her head. 'We had a tense time for a while when we couldn't locate the school bus but we have it now. One of the fishing boats has seen it from the sea. It's trapped on the cliff road round past the mines at the back of the island. There's been two landslips and the bus is trapped between them. As far as we know, they're all fine, but we're not going to be able to get them out until morning. Hence the airdrop. We'll drop a radio in, as well.'

'So it'll be okay.' Abby forced the words out. She had to believe them. It was about more than getting Jack back to a safe place. Much more.

Ginny was frowning at her now. Trust another woman to pick up on an undercurrent and wonder what was going on. Abby took a deep breath.

'They need you at the hospital.' Persuading Ben and Ginny to move on to where they were needed and allow herself and Tom to do the same was suddenly paramount. 'Here's Hannah. Ginny, is it okay if Button goes with her? You and Ginny are needed for medical stuff. Please, go fast. There are so many casualties. But Tom and I need to go now.' Abby moved away from his touch, leading the way. 'Let's go.'

Finally, they were airborne.

'We'll be there in no time, don't you worry.' Moz was happy to be doing something useful. He threw a grin sideways at Abby, who was sitting in the front of the helicopter but, from where he was sitting in the back, Tom could see that the reassurance hadn't softened the lines of tension in her face. She didn't say anything in response to Moz. She just nodded tersely and stared straight ahead into a dusk that was almost complete darkness.

Just as well the helicopter had a night sun. They could shine the powerful beam of light down onto the drop area and make it safe for Tom to winch down the supplies they were carrying. Or maybe even find a safe place to touch down. How happy would Abby be if she could bring her son on the return trip? No reason not to. They had plenty of room to include a small boy.

Her son.

His son.

Oh...God... For however long this short flight took, there was nothing else Tom needed to be doing. There was nothing to be talked about between the three people confined in this flying bubble. For the first time since this bombshell of news had landed on him, Tom was alone with his own thoughts.

Abby hadn't followed through with telling him she was pregnant. There was anger there. Lots of it. He'd had the right to know. He could have stepped up to the mark if he'd had the opportunity, but he'd simply been dismissed. Not even consulted.

What would have happened if he *had* known? How would he have reacted? If he was going to be honest with himself, Tom knew he probably wouldn't have reacted well. He'd never even considered taking on the responsibility of having kids. No way. Good grief, he'd broken up with Abby because she'd become an anchor.

Trying to hold him back from doing the job that was his life because it was dangerous. She'd only been his girl-friend. Having a family—a *child*—would have chained him to an even bigger anchor. There was no way it wouldn't have slowed him down. Clipped his wings.

No. He wouldn't have reacted well to the news. He would have been horrified. But he would have stepped up to the mark. He would have tried to make things work with Abby again and a part of him—maybe a huge part—would have been relieved to have her back in his life.

He'd missed her far more than he'd ever admitted, even to himself.

Moz was following the ribbon of the cliff road at a fairly low altitude. Tom could see the dark spikes of rocky coastline now that they were away from the beaches on the more inhabited side of Kaimotu Island. He could see the white foam of big waves breaking and the inky darkness of dense bush on the hills. This was wild country.

Beautiful but very isolated.

And this was where Abby had chosen to come to have her child. To raise him.

Not because she thought he'd make a terrible fa-ther, though.

Because she thought his son would have grown up thinking he was amazing. A hero.

A sensation Tom couldn't identify squeezed in his chest. Pride? Lots of people thought he was a hero. How many times had he had his photo in the paper or letters written to the rescue base praising his efforts to save the life of somebody's loved one? No, it was more than pride. It was something huge.

The idea of being loved by a child? That that child would learn to live with fear? A fear of losing *him*?

That was why Abby had been like she'd been about his job. Not initially, but after he'd been injured. She'd wanted him to be more careful. He'd seen it as her trying to clip his wings and hold him back because she didn't understand his passion and was trying to control him.

But she'd been scared.

The way she'd been scared about losing her adored parents.

Because…she'd loved him? *That* much?

Nobody had ever loved Tom that much. He hadn't wanted them to, had he?

It made life easier because you never had to get close enough to return a love that big, and that way you were never in any danger of being hurt by rejection.

Had he learned that lesson before he'd even been old enough to know what any of it was about? His teenage mother had never been in a position to raise him herself. As part of a huge, extended family, he'd been passed from household to household over the years. Always cared about. Loved, even, but somehow always on the periphery of the inner circle of family.

Maybe he'd coped with any sense of missing out by the adrenaline rush of danger that had always garnered attention. Being made a fuss of was a kind of love, wasn't it? That mechanism had started too early to remember, as well, but there was a photograph around of the cast he'd had on his broken arm when he'd fallen out of a tree, aged only two.

His mischief as a youngster had been the stuff of family legend. His exploits as an adult, after he'd discovered that taking risks was deemed far more acceptable if they were taken on behalf of others, attracted just as much attention. And all the women in his life had applauded his career, the same way that Abby had at the beginning of their relationship. Most of them, of the same ilk as Fizz, had urged him on to greater accomplishments. Bigger risks.

Because it wouldn't have mattered that much if he didn't come back?

Now Tom had another weird squeezing thing going on in his gut. Pretty much like the first one. He could see it wasn't pride, now. It was more a self-esteem thing. Feeling important. Not for the heroic or dangerous things you did for a job but simply because of who you were.

It was definitely a weird sensation and it was new but it wasn't entirely unpleasant.

'Almost there, Tank.' Moz was slowing the chopper. 'This looks like the first landslide coming up.'

Another glance down and Tom was again struck by the wildness of the landscape below.

He heard Abby's gasp as the bus came into view.

'Target sighted,' Moz said. 'We'll go around and get lower. Turning downwind.'

Abby's tension was palpable now, over and above the vibration of the helicopter. Every fibre of her being was focused on seeing her child. Making sure he was safe. Holding him in her arms, maybe.

Tom closed his eyes in a long blink. Imagine some-one caring so much about you that they took you to the most isolated place they could find to try and keep you safe?

Was Jack a lucky kid?

Or was he being suffocated?

He wouldn't want his son to grow up to be a sissy. Was he a frail kid? Was that why Abby was so wor-ried? Maybe he wore glasses and kept his nose buried in a book all day or too close to a computer screen for hours at a time.

Well…if that was the case, maybe Jack *did* need a father figure in his life. Maybe he wasn't too late to step up to that mark after all.

The chopper was much lower now. Hovering. It was time for Tom to do his job. To open the door and set up the winch to lower the parcel.

'Checking winch power,' he announced.

Moz turned on the night sun. They could see the bus and the crowd of children waving up at them. And the adults, who were keeping them well within a safe range. Abby was straining against her safety harness, focus-ing intently on the brightly lit scene below.

'Where is he?' she cried. 'I can't see Jack anywhere.'

'There's a lot of kids down there.' Moz sounded as calm as he always did. 'He'll be there somewhere. Speed back, Tank. Clear door.'

Abby was shaking her head. 'I'd see him, I know I would.'

'He might be inside the bus.' Tom was turning on the radio clipped to the outside of the blanket bundle. There was no way it could be missed, so they would be able to communicate clearly with the people on the ground within the next few minutes. 'We'll know pretty soon. Hang in there, Abby.'

He slid the side door open. 'Door back and locked,' he told Moz. 'Bringing hook inside.'

He attached the hook to the big parcel. 'Moving box to the door,' he informed Moz. Now he had to get permission to stand on the skids and control the winching process. 'Clear skids.'

'Clear skids,' Moz confirmed.

He had to make sure the parcel landed safely away from any people, which wasn't a simple process. Too far one way and the vital supplies, especially the radio, would go over the cliff and into the sea below. Dense bush on the other side of the cliff road could make it impossible for the people to find it in the dark.

There was enough clear road between the landslides, though. Enough to land on, except that it was a risk that wouldn't be deemed worth taking given the dangers on either side of the narrow road.

Tom watched the distance between the parcel hanging on the end of the winch line and the road below.

'Minus fifteen,' he told Moz. 'Ten…nine…eight…'

And then it was almost on the ground and the attachment was disengaged. Someone was running towards the parcel while others were keeping the children in a close knot beside the bus.

Tom picked up his radio.

'Hello?' he called. 'Hello, hello? Do you read?'

There was silence but he could see a man hunching over the big parcel. Reaching for the radio.

'Hello?' Tom tried again. 'Push the button on the top when you speak.'

A crackling noise came through, along with the end of an unintelligible sentence.

'Try again,' Tom directed. 'Hold the button and keep it down. Can you hear me?'

'Yes...' The word was a shout.

'You have food and blankets. We're looking at ways of getting you out but it won't be till daylight, now. Is there anything else you require urgently?'

'Yes.'

Tom was aware of Abby twisting in her seat. Of her eyes widening. An urgent message was coming silently.

Ask about Jack.... Please, Tom.

'What's the problem?' Tom had to stay professional here. He couldn't single out a particular child to ask about, even if was his own son.

'We have a child missing.' The man had figured out the radio now. 'He was still in the old copper mine when the quake struck and the walls collapsed at the entrance.'

'Only one child?'

'Yes. A teacher has stayed behind. We could hear him calling.'

'Is he injured?'

'Don't think so. Don't know. We came on the bus to get help and that's when we got stuck. It's not far to the mine from here but we decided it was too dangerous to send anyone back. It's been hours...'

Tom didn't need to hear how hard it was for Abby to control her breathing right now. He knew the answer to his question before he even asked.

'Who's the child?'

'Jack Miller. He's only five, poor little guy. Just started school a few weeks ago.'

Tom heard a low oath from Moz underscoring a stifled sob from Abby. He took another look at the stretch of road between the landslips.

The risk might not have been justifiable a few minutes ago but there was no question about it now.

'Take us down, Moz,' Tom said quietly. 'We're needed here.'

CHAPTER FIVE

ABBY HELD HER BREATH as the helicopter came down to land on the narrow road in the dark. She wished she had a hand to hold.

Tom's hand?

She could see how intently Moz was concentrating on controlling the aircraft so she knew this was not an easy task. It could be that it was actually far more dangerous than she knew. She didn't want to know. She just wanted to be on the ground.

Moving.

She had to get to Jack. Her own safety was almost irrelevant at this moment.

'Good job, mate.' There was a note in Tom's voice as they touched down and the rotors began to slow that suggested to Abby that she had been right in thinking that this landing had been dangerous. They'd taken a risk here.

Because Tom had suggested it?

Abby's flash of gratitude was swiftly displaced by the desperate need to get out of the helicopter. To find a way to reach that mine and start searching for Jack. She fumbled with the clasp on her safety harness. It was Tom who reached through from the back and re-leased the catches.

'Follow me,' he directed. 'And keep your head down. The rotors haven't stopped.'

'Why not?' Abby's head turned sharply back in the pilot's direction. 'You're coming, too, aren't you, Moz? We need all the help we can get.'

Moz and Tom exchanged a long glance. And then Moz reached to flick some switches and Abby heard the engine noise change. It was shutting down.

'I'm in.' Moz nodded. 'I'll grab what we've got in the way of ropes and stuff. You guys go and get briefed.'

The man who'd retrieved the air-drop parcel and the radio was waiting for them. Dennis Smythe, born and bred on Kaimotu Island, was the senior teacher of the junior school. Usually laid back and well in control of any trouble a bunch of kids could manufacture, he looked anguished right now.

'Abby, I'm *so* sorry. I can't believe this has happened to Jack, of all people...'

Words were torn from Abby. '*How* did it happen?'

'We were getting on the bus to come back to school. He was right at the end of the line. Apparently he re-alised he'd dropped something when we were exploring and he was off like a little rocket back into the mine to try and find it. His teacher, Shelley, tried to stop him but couldn't so I took off after him, but that was when the quake hit. I...I was thrown off my feet. The kids were all panicking... It was complete chaos for a bit.'

Abby could only nod. She would never forget those interminable seconds of the initial quake. The terror of feeling like the world was in the process of ending.

'We could hear Jack calling,' Dennis continued. 'Just faintly. We couldn't get inside the entrance because the beams had come down with a ton of rocks and other stuff. We knew we needed help but the phones weren't working.'

'The tower came down.' Abby was trying hard to listen but the information was coming too slowly and there wasn't enough of it. But she could see how hard this was hitting Dennis and, whatever had happened, it hadn't been his fault. He'd had the responsibility for a lot of people, most of them children, and she knew he would have done his absolute best.

'We decided the quickest way to get help would be to take the bus and we needed to get the others to safety, as well. Shelley volunteered to stay at the mine so she could try and talk to Jack and keep him reassured that help was on its way.'

'What…what was he calling? Is…is he hurt?'

'Shelley didn't think so. He was scared, of course. He…he was calling for you, Abby. Calling "Mummy"…'

'Oh…oh, *God*…' Abby had to press a hand to her eyes. She felt Tom step closer and felt his arm go around her. The touch was starting to feel familiar again and it was an offer of strength she couldn't refuse. Abby leaned into him and tried so hard not to give in to the tears that wanted to come that she could feel her whole body trembling.

'Tell us everything you can,' Tom instructed. 'How well do you know this area?'

'Like the back of my hand,' Dennis told him. 'I grew up here, mate. Right below here is the beach that was the best place on the island for some serious surfing.

There's a track that leads down the cliff somewhere close. And a jetty. I reckon we could get these kids out by boat but I wouldn't try it in the dark. No way.'

'How do we get to the mine? Along the shore?'

'No, that wouldn't work. There's only one track and you can't get back up past the bay. I reckon you'll need to get into the bush and head up. You could clear the slip where it started and then get back down to the road. Couple of kilometres on and you'll find the road to the mines. It's signposted. Or it was, anyway...' Dennis started to rub his forehead. 'I don't know if anything's like it's supposed to be anymore. What's happened in town? Has anybody been hurt? I've been worried sick about Suzie. She's pregnant, you know. About three months along.'

Abby took a deep breath. A very deep breath. Dennis and Suzie had married only last year.

'It's bad, Dennis, but a lot of help's arrived from the mainland. Experts, like Tom here. I haven't seen or heard anything about Suzie but that's a good thing. It probably means she's okay. Tom, will the radio work to contact someone like Mike Henley?'

'Yes. I just need to change the channel being used.'

'Can you do that now? There must be so many parents who're desperate to know their children are okay and then...and then can we get going? To the mine?'

It was dark now and Tom's eyes were dark anyway so Abby shouldn't have been able to see his expression of complete understanding so easily.

Other parents were desperate, yes, but they were about to find out their children were safe. To be able to talk to them even, maybe.

She was the only one who couldn't get that reassurance.

Yet.

But there was more than sympathy in that gaze. There was the reassurance that only Tom could give her right now.

We'll find him, Abby, the look told her. *We can do this. Everything's going to be okay.*

There had been a point in Abby's life when she had trusted Tom absolutely. But he had broken that trust when he'd ended their relationship. Broken her heart. Could she believe in him again? Trust what that look was telling her?

Yes, she could. She *had* to.

Moz had coils of rope over his shoulders and a backpack stuffed with everything else he could find that might be useful.

Tom tightened the straps on his backpack, which contained all the medical supplies they might need.

Abby was given a pack with a couple of blankets and some of the food and water they'd brought there.

They all had hard hats on with lamps that were now glowing. Heavy boots that would help them cope with the terrain. Overalls that would help protect them from superficial injury. And determination that they were going to succeed on this unexpected mission.

They were all grateful for the overalls as they pushed their way uphill through native bush that had a dense undergrowth of scratchy punga ferns. They kept as close as they could to the side of the slip and eventually came to where the land had been shaken loose and had started the slide. The trees above still seemed soundly rooted and gave them a secure passage to the other side and then they had to get down the steep hillside again, slipping frequently and catching themselves on nearby tree trunks. Once, Abby missed a catch and fell, sliding a long way before coming up against a larger fern.

Tom's heart skipped a beat. He was by her side in seconds, helping her as she struggled back to her feet.

'Are you okay?'

'I'm fine. Keep going, Tom. I'm *fine*.'

She wasn't. She may not have been injured by the fall but she wasn't fine. How could she be?

Abby knew her son was in danger. Possibly trapped and hurt. She'd just fought her way up a slope that had been enough to drain Tom's energy but she'd refused a water stop at the top. She was hurtling downhill now and it would have been that speed and determination that had made her slip in the first place.

But she wasn't about to stop. Or even slow down, thank you very much.

She was fearless right now. A woman who was going to do whatever it took to save someone she loved. She was staring at him, still radiating that fierce resolve to carry on.

The direct beam of Tom's headlamp pointed above her head but Abby was bathed in the surrounding circle of light.

She was filthy. Her overalls were splattered with the same mud that streaked her face. The long plait of her blonde hair was coming unravelled and was festooned with twigs and pieces of fern frond. A deep scratch on her cheek was adding blood to the grime. Any vestige of make-up she'd been wearing had long since vanished.

But her eyes shone with determination and an inner strength that Tom had never recognised in Abby. And her lips trembled with a vulnerability that he'd also never known about because she'd kept it so well buried.

At this moment, in possibly the most isolated place in which he'd ever been, Abby Miller was *the* most beautiful woman Tom had ever laid eyes on.

And there was that odd squeezy sensation in his chest again. The same as he'd got in the wake of imagining someone loving him so much they couldn't bear anything bad happening to him. The same, only different, because it was like he was transmitting that sensation now instead of simply receiving it.

He didn't want anything bad to happen to Abby. He wanted to protect her.

But he also wanted to cheer her on.

Maybe *this* was pride. He was proud of Abby.

His breath felt ragged as he dragged it in. Was his hand actually shaking as he reached out to check whether that cut on Abby's cheek needed attention before they carried on?

'What's up, Tank?' Moz's voice carried easily from a fair way further down the slope. 'I think I can see the road again.'

Abby pulled her face away from the touch of Tom's fingers. With even more of an effort she pulled her gaze away from what she could see in his eyes.

Admiration?

Tenderness, even?

She could have drowned in that look. Just as well, the sound of Moz's voice carried so clearly.

'It can wait,' she told Tom. 'It's just a scratch.'

Her knee could wait, too, even though it was hurting badly now. By the time they reached the road it was getting hard to disguise the fact that she couldn't put her whole weight on that leg. What would Tom do if he saw her limping?

Carry her to where her son was?

Probably.

She couldn't let that happen. She couldn't let herself be dependent on Tom in any way.

Not physically. And definitely not emotionally. Dear Lord…even under these circumstances, that touch of his fingers on her face had woken memories that had pushed insistently into her mind as she'd walked on.

The way he'd once played with her toes, for example, when they'd been curled up on a couch together, watching television. Idle touching that would morph into a truly excellent foot massage until they both lost interest in the movie and her feet would be neglected in favour of more exciting parts of her body for him to touch.

The way he'd held her head when they'd kissed, with his fingers woven through her hair and pressing onto her scalp.

The way he would lie beside her, when they were both completely naked, usually in the aftermath of making love, and he would use his fingertips so gently. He would trace the entire outline of her body as if he was drawing her shape in sand. Or committing it to memory.

How could a single touch unleash so many memories? Abby had had no idea they were still lurking so close to the surface. She had to bury them and make sure they were deep enough this time. She had to protect herself.

She could do this. Shut the memories away and not react to any touch, accidental or otherwise. And she'd make sure she didn't start depending on Tom. Not emotionally and not physically.

Not even as a co-parent.

He might think he wanted to get involved in Jack's life now but how long would that last? How available would he be if some exciting mission came up? What if Jack was holding his breath, waiting for his dad to make an appearance at a school play or a prizegiving and Tom didn't show up because he'd been called back to work or his helicopter happened to have crashed on that particular day?

Oh…good grief…

Abby allowed enough of her weight to go onto her bad knee to send a sharp twinge right through her body as a kind of wake-up call.

As if she didn't have enough to worry about right now. Yet here she was, imagining a worst-case scenario for something in a future that wasn't even on the horizon. Tom hadn't even met his son. He certainly hadn't said anything about wanting to be a part of their lives.

They had turned off the main cliff road now, where the signpost to the tourist attraction of the old copper mine was still standing, albeit at a drunken angle.

Maybe it was some kind of a defence mechanism, Abby excused herself. By looking into the future, perhaps she was giving herself the reassurance that they would get through the tension and fear of their present situation.

That Jack would be okay and he'd go on to do a school play or excel at something enough to be deemed worthy of a special prize. Not that she needed him to win any prizes. All she wished for was that her little boy would be safe. And grow up happy.

So why did she invent disasters for the future? Was she incapable of imagining something wonderful?

Like…like Jack getting his first puppy, for instance. His face shining with joy. His dad on the floor beside him, playing with the pup and offering silly suggestions for names. His mum there, too. Taking pictures to add to the family album. Laughing at the puppy's antics. Knowing that this happy moment would become a treasured memory.

Abby's breath escaped in something far too close to a sob.

This was why she conjured up disasters and not joyful moments. Because the pain of knowing those moments would never happen was too much.

The longing *hurt*, dammit. And, right now, it was worse than ever because he was here. And he'd touched her face as if he cared and it had made her remember too much.

Tom had slowed his pace. He'd heard that sound of distress she'd been unable to stifle.

'You're limping.' The words were an accusation.

'I'm fine.'

'Dammit, Abby. Be honest for once. What's hurting?'

Abby almost laughed aloud. He wanted her to be

honest? If he knew what had really hurt her, he'd run a mile.

That joyous glimpse into an imaginary future for her would no doubt represent a disaster for Tom Kendrick. A family hanging around his neck like a millstone. Holding him back from the adrenaline rush of hurling himself into danger at every opportunity. Of being a real-life hero. Admired by all and loved by many.

That sweet-little-puppy scenario she'd lost herself in for a few moments wasn't going to happen. Not in this lifetime.

'It's my knee,' was what she did say. 'I gave it a bump, way back, when the earthquake first happened. It's just getting a bit stiff now, that's all.'

Moz had come back to where Tom was walking more slowly beside Abby.

'How far have we still got to go?' he asked.

'I'm not sure,' Abby said. 'Not too far, I think.'

For a minute or two the three of them walked in silence.

'Hey…' The call was female. And faint. 'Is someone there? I can see a light. Help…we're up here. *Help*…'

Tom's voice rang out clearly in the night air. 'We're coming,' he shouted. 'Hold on…'

The teacher who had stayed behind at the mine, Shelley Carter, was young, in her early twenties. By now she'd been alone out here for many hours. She was exhausted and scared and when she saw Moz, Tom and Abby arriving, she burst into tears.

It took a while for Tom to be sure she wasn't injured

in any way and to get the information he needed to start assessing the situation.

'It wasn't so bad while it was still light.' Wrapped in a blanket now and drinking a bottle of water from the supplies they had brought with them, Shelley was finally calm enough to talk, although her voice was very hoarse. 'The aftershocks were really scary but I could keep busy, you know? And I could talk to Jack. Well, yell at him, anyway...' She drank some more water. 'I've almost lost my voice.'

The first thing Abby had done when they'd arrived at the scene had been to get as close as she could to the entrance and start calling.

'Jack? Jack, can you hear me, darling? Mummy's here. We're all here to rescue you. Jack? *Jack?*'

There'd been no response to her calls and Abby had stopped for now. She was standing nearby, her arms wrapped around her body, her bottom lip caught between her teeth, staring at Shelley as she talked.

From where he was crouched beside Shelley, Tom glanced up at Abby and then back to the young teacher.

'How long ago did you last hear Jack?' he asked quietly.

Shelley shook her head. 'I'm not sure. I've kind of lost track of time, you know? I guess it was after it got dark. I had to stop trying to shift rocks and stuff. And I couldn't yell as loudly because I was already starting to lose my voice.'

Abby's head flicked back and the light from her helmet raked over the blocked entrance to the mine. Another light was moving further away as Moz explored the site.

'Maybe...maybe he fell asleep,' Shelley whispered. But fresh tears rolled down her face. She was thinking exactly what had gone through Tom's mind and what he knew would be filling Abby's.

That Jack might be unconscious rather than asleep. Lying inside that mine somewhere, badly hurt. Dying, even...

Tom heard Abby suck in a breath.

'What made him go back inside like that?'

'Action...Man,' Shelley gulped.

Abby groaned. 'I *told* him he couldn't take him to school. He must have hidden him inside his school bag when I wasn't looking.'

'What are we talking about here?' Tom was frowning. Why had Jack disobeyed his mother? Was he a naughty kid?

Because he didn't have a father around?

'Action Man.' Abby shook her head. 'It was his birthday present when he turned five. He'd been desperate for one.'

'It's a toy? A...a *doll*?' Oh, man, this was getting worse.

'Kind of.' But Abby had a poignant smile tugging at the corner of her mouth. 'It's an action figure. Special operations kind of hero doll and you can bend the joints to do almost anything. Action Man can climb table legs and abseil off the top of doors and parachute out of trees. He can do pretty much everything a little boy can dream of being able to do himself, I guess.'

Ohh...

Tom found himself smiling. If he'd had a doll like that when he'd been a kid, maybe he wouldn't have collected so many bumps and bruises and broken bones trying stuff out for himself.

'Tank?' Moz was still a short distance away. 'Come and have a look over here.'

'Tank?' Shelley looked at Abby as Tom pushed himself upright. 'I thought his name was Tom?'

'It is,' Abby responded. 'Tank's a nickname. You know, like Thomas the Tank Engine?'

Tom heard Shelley giggle behind him. 'That's what we need,' she said to Abby. 'A real-life Action Man.'

Tom strode towards where Moz was. That odd little smile was still curling one side of his mouth. Because Abby had remembered his nickname?

No. It was more like he could imagine a little boy making his toy climb a table leg. Maybe making him talk at the same time. Being so attached to that toy that he'd rebelled against his mother's orders and sneaked him into a hiding place in his school bag. Clearly, his worry that Jack was a sissy was unfounded. He was starting to get a picture of what Jack was like.

His son was becoming a real person....

'Look.' Moz directed the beam of his headlamp. 'There's a gap here where the beams have crossed. If we shift a few rocks, we might be able to get access.'

How dangerous would that be? How precarious was any space left inside this mine entrance? How many aftershocks were still to come and how strong would they be? Enough to bring another load of rocks and earth down to bury any gaps?

One of those gaps contained his son.

'Let's do it.' Tom had already positioned himself beside one of the larger boulders. He put his shoulder against it and waited until Moz joined him. 'Ready? On the count of three. One...two...*three*...'

Abby was beside them by the time the boulder had rolled clear.

'Oh, my God...' she gasped. 'There's a *gap*.'

'Stay clear,' Tom ordered. 'We don't know which way these rocks are going to roll. You can come and have a look when there's something to see, okay?'

It took a remarkably short time for the two men to shift the boulders and the gap was easily big enough for them to get inside. Tom would have preferred to keep Abby well out until they'd assessed how safe it was but she was having none of it.

Shelley was more than happy to stay where she was, wrapped up in her blanket, but Abby was right behind them as they entered the pitch blackness of the old mine entrance.

Only the beams around the end of the tunnel seemed to have collapsed. Inside, the roof and walls still had their tunnel shape. A few rocks had fallen further in but there was enough space to climb over them. They still couldn't see what lay ahead.

'Jack?' His voice bounced off the wall and echoed in the tunnel as Tom shouted. 'Jack? Can you hear me?'

'*Jack*...' Abby yelled as soon as Tom stopped. 'Jack, where are you?'

She hauled in a breath to call again but Tom gripped her arm. 'Shh...'

Abby's jaw dropped in shock but then he saw that she understood. If they kept yelling themselves, they wouldn't be able to hear a response, especially if it was faint.

And there it was. Very faint. Sounding sleepy.
'Mummy...?'

Abby's head swivelled so that she could catch Tom's gaze.

Had she really heard what she thought she'd heard?

Tom gave an imperceptible nod and Abby pressed a fist to her mouth. Trying to control herself so that she wouldn't burst into tears of relief? She was still holding his gaze and Tom could feel his own throat closing over a rather large lump. What he couldn't decide was whether that was due to the sound of that small voice or the relief he was feeling because Abby was so relieved.

She was still scared, though. And he was still holding her arm. He gave it a squeeze to encourage her. She would want to sound strong for Jack. She wouldn't want him to know how scared she was.

'Yes...' The word came out as a whisper so Abby had to try again. 'Mummy's here, Jack. We're coming to get you. Are you...? Does anything hurt?'

'I'm cold, Mummy. I want to go *home.*'

'I know, darling.' Tom could see that Abby had her eyes shut now. He could see the way her lips trembled when she wasn't talking but, amazingly, she was sounding incredibly strong. Confident. 'It won't be long now. We're coming to get you, okay?'

A faint sobbing could be heard now. *'Mum—mee...'*

The sound of Jack's voice was faint enough to be coming from a long way into the mine. Just how far had they taken the children exploring? Or had Jack missed where he'd dropped his toy and kept running in panic during or after the earthquake?

Abby was moving forward now, eager to find Jack. It was Moz who yelled a warning.

'Abby, *stop...*'

She turned her head towards Moz so she wasn't looking where she was going. Thank God her steps had faltered at the warning because Tom's light now zeroed in on what lay ahead. Where the floor of the tunnel simply disappeared.

His heart in his throat, he launched himself towards Abby, catching her in his arms and hauling her backwards.

'What the—?' Abby struggled in his hold. 'Tom, let me *go.*'

Tom had to struggle to take a normal breath, waiting for his heart to get back to a normal rhythm.

'Abby.' He kept his tone as calm as he could. 'Look...'

Abby looked. She sagged in his arms, and knowing that she could now see the danger, Tom let her go. Let her sink to her knees and stare over the edge of where the floor of the tunnel simply stopped.

'There must have been another tunnel running beneath this one.' It was Moz who spoke first. 'Something's given way to create this sinkhole.'

'How far does it go?' Abby's voice was shaking. 'And how do we get down?'

Tom's heart sank. How could he tell her that they had no idea how deep the hole was? Or how stable the sides of it were? That any movement could send a pile of earth and rocks cascading down to bury both Jack and anyone who was crazy enough to climb down?

He couldn't, that's all there was to it.

'I'll go down with a rope,' he said quietly. 'And see how far I can get.'

'Uh…Tank…' Moz's tone was a clear warning. He knew how far out of any acceptable protocol Tom was stepping.

'Can you anchor the rope?' Tom didn't give Moz the chance to voice any doubts. He used his headlamp to survey the surroundings. 'We'll use that beam, there. That'll hold most of my weight. You'll just need to feed me the length.'

Silently Moz took a long coil of rope from his shoulder and the two men moved to set up. Abby stayed by the edge of the hole.

'We're coming, Jack. Did…did you find Action Man?'

'No-o-o…'

'Doesn't matter, darling. We'll get you a new one, I promise.'

'But I want *my* Action Man.'

Tom had one end of the rope secured around his waist. Moz had another section of it around his own waist. Between them, the rope snaked around the solid beam that was part of the tunnel support.

'You sure about this, mate?'

Tom simply turned away and walked to the edge of the hole. Of course he was sure. It was his son who was at the bottom of that hole.

The walls were sloping to start with and it wasn't difficult to climb down. The rope was only needed as insurance so far but the danger was an unknown quantity and Tom moved very carefully. When his foot sent a shower of dirt and a small rock plunging down, he stopped and held his breath.

'*Jack?*' Abby shouted from above. 'Are you okay? Did anything hit you?'

'No...' came the small voice. 'It's okay, Mummy. I've got a roof.'

A *roof*?

Tom inched his way down until he could go no further. He was at a point where the huge beams from the tunnel above had wedged themselves in a criss-cross pattern across the hole, leaving only a small gap in the middle.

They seemed solid enough. Tom knelt on one of them to peer through. His lamp lit up a kind of rough cavern beneath. At least twenty feet further down he could see a jumble of rocks and piles of earth. But nothing else.

'Jack?' His voice felt weird and the name of his son came out too faint to be useful. He cleared his throat. 'Jack? Can you hear me, buddy?'

Silence. And then something pale appeared in the dark shape of a huddled child amongst the boulders as a small face turned up towards the light.

'Who're you?' A frightened little voice.

'I'm...'

I'm your dad, Jack.

'I'm Tom...a friend of your mum's. I've come to get you out of here.'

Except there was no way he could get down to Jack. No way in the world he could push his huge frame through the only available gap. They needed help from engineers, here. Some heavy-duty equipment, which might have to be brought over to the island from the mainland. Diggers. Cranes. Oh, God. How long would that take?

Abby's headlamp was shining on the same place his was.

'What's the problem, Tom?'

'I can't get through the gap. It's too small.'

'Jack's small. Can't he climb up to it?'

Tom had to swallow hard. 'No. He's a good twenty feet further down and he wouldn't manage the climb.'

'I could get through that gap.'

'No way, Abby. It's far too dangerous. Stay where you are.' The beam he was cautiously kneeling on was solid enough but Tom wasn't about to push his luck any further. He could feel a sponginess that instinct told him was a very clear warning. One good aftershock and this whole lot could shake loose and tumble further.

No way on earth was he going to let Abby risk her life here.

Tom turned his attention back to what lay between him and rescuing Jack. Could he find another gap? Somehow move one of these beams?

He reached out to test the earth around where one end of a beam was wedged. The dirt crumbled in his fingers and, weirdly, some of it seemed to fly up and ping off his helmet.

Tom stopped what he was doing.

Another shower of earth rained down. A small stone sounded like the graze of a bullet on his helmet.

Realisation hit far too late.

Appalled, Tom looked up again but he knew he wouldn't see the beam of Abby's headlamp where it had been.

She was already halfway down the slope of the sink-hole, without even the protection of a rope. He saw the moment the small boulder she was using as a hand grip came loose from the surrounding earth.

The moment that Abby began to slip.

CHAPTER SIX

IT HAPPENED TOO FAST to feel any fear.

That reaction came seconds later, kicking in the moment Abby felt the grip of Tom's arms as he caught her and stopped her fall. When she realised she was safe, in that powerful hold, hearing the fervent relief in the oath that escaped Tom's lips, along with her name.

'Abby...'

As if *her* safety was the most important thing here. The way he said her name touched something very deep but Abby could ignore it far more easily than that touch on her face a while back. It wasn't *her* safety that mattered. And, anyway, she was relatively safe again now. More importantly, her impulsive action of climbing into the sinkhole hadn't made things worse. What if she'd dislodged enough debris to send the whole lot crashing down to bury Jack?

Jack.

Abby pushed the fear aside. Wrenched herself out of Tom's arms so that she could drop to her knees and put her face into that gap between the beams.

She could *see* him.

And he looked so small and vulnerable. Dirty and

scared and all hunched up in a little ball. Somehow Abby choked back a sob and even managed to sound calm.

'Hey, sweetheart…'

'Mummy.' Jack started to cry. 'Can we go home now? I d-don't like it down here.'

'I know, darling. You just hold on tight. We're going to get you out of there.'

'Abby…' The way Tom said her name this time was very different. A warning rather than a prayer of thanks. A warning that she was promising something they couldn't deliver?

'I can get through that gap,' she told Tom. 'I'm sure I can.'

'And then what?' Tom kept his voice low so that Jack couldn't overhear. 'Drop twenty feet and break your leg? So that we've got two people to try and dig out?'

'You're not using your rope. You can tie that around me.'

'No. I won't let you do this, Abby. It's far too dangerous. We have no idea how stable any of this stuff is. We'll radio for backup. Get some engineers and USAR guys here.'

'And how long will that take?'

They both knew the answer to that. *Too long.*

'You can't stop me, Tom.'

'Oh, I can, Abby.' It was more than a warning now. More like a threat.

'That's my *son* down there,' Abby hissed.

Tom just stared at her silently. He didn't have to say it. It was *his* son down there, too.

As if nature was impatient with the stand-off, a rumble of sound echoed in the mine shaft and the ground shook. It wasn't a big aftershock but it was enough to remind them all of how they came to be here in the first place. Of just how dangerous it was. That they all needed to get out of there as fast as possible and the clock was ticking loudly.

Abby had to bite her lip hard to stop herself crying out in fear. Jack screamed. Tom's face was grimmer than she'd ever seen it. Even when he'd been lying in his hospital bed, telling her that their relationship was over. That it could never work so the best thing for both of them would be to walk away now before anybody got really hurt.

It had been way too late for her by then. It wasn't too late now but it soon could be. For Jack. And for them. Was Tom going to learn that he was a father and then lose his child on the very same day?

No. It wasn't going to happen. Abby wasn't going to let it happen. She'd rather die trying to prevent it.

'You can't do this, Abby.' Tom's tone was curiously hollow.

'I can't *not* do it,' was her response.

'You guys okay down there?' Moz was at the rim of the sinkhole, the rope he'd been monitoring wrapped around his waist instead of the beam, now.

'So far,' Tom said grimly. 'Chuck that rope down here, will you, Moz? Abby's going to try and get down to get Jack.'

'*What?* Oh, man…' Moz sounded shocked.

'Just do it,' Tom ordered. 'Chuck the rope.'

Moz did it silently. Maybe nobody argued with Tom when he used that commanding tone. Abby wasn't about to, either. Not when he was knotting the rope into a kind of harness and giving her instructions about how she could use the underside of the criss-crossing beams to get to where she could find a foothold to help her get down to the bottom of the sinkhole.

There was no going back as she squeezed herself through the tight gap between the beams. Having achieved that, she found herself suspended in midair, groping for a handhold to start trying to move sideways. The rope bit painfully under her arms and between her legs. The dank smell of damp earth filled her nostrils and she had no way of knowing whether anything she held on to would be strong enough to take her weight. Or whether the earth would start moving again, and that would simply be the end of it all.

Abby had never done anything this dangerous in her whole life. It would have been impossibly terrifying if it wasn't for the fact that she was doing this to get to Jack. Having been compelled to start and now on her way, however, she couldn't deny the underlying thrill that was interlaced with the terror. The adrenaline rush was unexpectedly powerful. Exhilarating, even.

And it certainly helped that she had Tom watching her back. Keeping his headlamp where it was needed and talking her quietly through the ordeal.

'There's a rock…to your left…down about a foot.'

'Stay where you are. Catch your breath.'

'You can do this, Abby. You'll have to jump the last bit. I can take some of your weight so you'll land softly.'

Then she was down.

Checking Jack out all over. 'Are you sure nothing hurts? Nothing at all?'

'No. I just want to go home.'

Abby's voice wobbled. 'Not before I get a squeezy hug.'

Tears came then, but only a few. The clock was ticking even more loudly in this potential tomb. They had
to get out in case another, larger aftershock happened.

'How will we do this, Tom?' Abby called. 'Do I take
my harness off and put it on Jack?'

'No-o-o...' Jack might consider himself to be getting
too big for squeezy hugs but he clung to Abby fiercely
now. 'Don't put me down, Mummy. *Don't.*'

'I'll send down another rope,' Tom called back. 'You
can put it round Jack but we won't use it unless we have
to. Do you think you can climb back up while you're
holding him?'

'Yes.' Abby made sure she sounded confident but
she had no idea whether she was capable of doing this.
She swallowed hard and put her mouth close to Jack's
ear. She could feel his warmth. The tickle of his soft
hair against her face.

She was halfway towards succeeding in what had
seemed like an impossible mission such a short time
ago. There was more than the thrill of the danger, now.
Abby could sense how overwhelming it would be when
they got through this and were safe again.

'You'll have to help me, Jack. You'll have to hang
on like a little monkey so I can use my hands to help
us climb. Like...like Action Man would. Can you do
that, do you think?'

Jack nodded but his bottom lip wobbled. 'I couldn't
find Action Man,' he said sadly.

The end of the new rope was dangling above her now.
Abby wound it around Jack and tied the best knots she
knew how. If, God forbid, she fell or dropped him on

the way up, Tom would be able to save him. 'It doesn't matter,' she told Jack as she worked. 'We'll get you another Action Man.'

'But he won't be *mine.*'

Abby was already moving. She hitched her son more securely against her body. 'Hold on really, really tight,' she instructed. 'This is the biggest squeezy hug you're ever going to have to give me, okay?'

'Okay.'

It was much harder getting back up, with the extra weight of Jack. Painful, too, with the rope continuing to bite into her body from the moment Tom had used his weight to help her up that first bit, which she'd jumped on the way down. Was he trying to make it easier by taking some of the weight?

By the time Abby got up to the level of the wedged beams, she could hear that Moz had joined Tom in the hole. Why? Surely they needed someone up on solid ground in the tunnel in case something went wrong?

And then she realised why both men had put themselves in more danger. This was the point where she had to let go of Jack because there was no way she could fit back through that gap while she was holding him. Tom was lying above the gap and he had his head and arms through it.

'Moz has got Jack's rope, Abby. You need to hold him out. Jack? You need to grab my hands, buddy, so I can pull you up.'

'No-o-o...' Jack clung more tightly. 'Don't let me go, Mummy.'

'I have to, baby. Just for a few seconds. And then it'll

be my turn to come through the hole and I'll never let you go again if you don't want me to. Okay?'

'*N-o-o-o.*' Jack was sobbing. Terrified.

'Tom's my special friend,' Abby said desperately. 'He's your...' *Dad.* The word so very nearly slipped out. 'That makes him *your* special friend, too. He won't let anything bad happen to you, I promise.' She was prising Jack's arms and legs from around her body, unaware of the tears coursing down her face. 'Tom's like...he's a real-life Action Man, Jack. This is what he does. He saves people.'

Jack's sob ended on a hiccup. He'd turned his head to see if he could see this real-life Action Man. All either of them could see was the blinding glare of the headlamp, of course, and the two big hands waiting to catch hold of Jack, but having his attention diverted even for a moment was enough for Abby to break the hold.

She lifted her son away from her body and turned him to face outwards. She stretched her arms out to the limit of their capacity. Holding her baby over what now seemed like a huge, huge drop.

Jack shrieked in terror but his arms had gone out instinctively to find something to hold on to. Instead, Tom's hands had circled the small wrists.

'Pull us back, Moz.'

Abby saw Jack's little legs disappear through the gap. She was shaking like a leaf now. No way could she manage to get over there and back through that gap by herself.

She didn't need to. A moment later she felt the rope around her body tighten.

'Your turn, Abby. I've got you. I won't let you fall.'

It only seemed a blink of time since Abby had been trying so hard to hide the fact that she was limping so that Tom wouldn't notice. So that he wouldn't scoop her up and make life easier for her. Since she had resolved so firmly not to allow herself to depend on this man again. Somewhere in the back of her mind, now, there was an echo of something that could have been an ironic chuckle. Who had she been trying to kid?

She was dependent on him for her very life at this moment and she knew without a shadow of doubt that she could trust him. There was nobody else alive that she could give this kind of trust to.

So, when he had taken her whole weight and pulled her to the relative safety of the other side of that gap, it seemed only natural that he would keep pulling until he had her so tightly clasped in his arms it seemed like he never intended to let her go.

And it was just as natural that breaking such awful tension would release a flood of emotion from Abby. That she was laughing and crying at the same time. Holding Tom just as tightly as he was holding her. That his head was bent over hers and they were pressed so close together that when she moved her head, her lips brushed Tom's cheek. That when his head moved in response, it was their lips that brushed.

The intensity of the emotions spiked to become utterly confusing. Overwhelming. Not that there was any time to process any of it. Moz was right there beside them. And Jack, who sounded more scared now than he had at the bottom of the hole.

'Why are you crying, Mummy? What's the matter?'

Did Tom's hold soften or had Abby wrenched herself free? She couldn't tell. The need to touch her son was overwhelming.

'Nothing's the matter, darling. I'm just happy that we're out of the big hole. That we're safe.'

'We'll be a lot safer when we get right out of this damn tunnel.' Tom's voice was a growl. 'Let's move.'

The anger should have evaporated long ago.

The relief of getting Abby back through that gap should have been almost enough. Getting all three of them out of the sinkhole with assistance from Moz certainly should have done it.

But it hadn't.

Tom was at the rear of the small procession finally making its way out of the mine shaft. He knew he had been far too curt in ordering everybody to get moving but this wasn't the place for celebrating success. They could do that when they were safely clear of a space that could close in on them with a decent aftershock.

Why was he still so damned *angry*?

Maybe it was just a kind of chemical reaction. There were too many, powerful emotions roiling around inside him and, because they were all mixed together, they were producing an explosive heat. Did it just *feel* like anger because he had no other yardstick to measure it by?

He'd certainly *been* angry. With Abby, for refusing to listen to reason and putting herself into such a dangerous situation. With himself, because he'd had no choice but to allow her to in the end. She'd been right. Trying to save Jack had been a no-brainer. It couldn't *not* be done. And she'd been the only person physically capable of fitting through that gap.

And she'd done it. She was amazing. He should be full of admiration for her courage. Pride, because she wasn't a stranger and he had the right to be proud of her. Relief, because she hadn't been killed and he didn't have to face the prospect of never seeing her again for as long as he lived.

Was that why he was so angry?

Because he still *loved* Abby?

He'd never felt anything like when he'd pulled her through that gap and had kept pulling until he'd had her as close as it was possible to have anybody who was fully clothed in rescue gear. He had felt Abby's heart pounding against his chest. Against his own heart. He'd felt the huff of her breath as she'd sobbed with relief and the tight grip of her arms around his neck. He'd felt the sweet brush of her lips against his cheek and then the explosion of sensation when they'd touched *his* lips.

An accidental kiss?

Of course it had been. But if he'd needed a slap in the face to wake him up, it had certainly done the trick. Of course he still loved Abby.

The knowledge had been waiting to punch him from the first moment he'd seen her in that waiting room, hadn't it?

Had he really thought it was simply ancient history? That he'd buried his feelings for Abby so well, along with everything else about that break-up, that it had become impenetrable?

And now there was Jack.

It had been Tom who'd carried the small boy out of

the sinkhole. In his arms. He could still feel the clutch of those skinny arms around his neck. The sturdy little legs around his waist. He was such a small person. So incredibly vulnerable.

He hadn't been crying, though. He was just as brave as his mother.

Maybe just as brave as his father?

Oh…man… Yes. These feelings were overwhelming. The build-up of pressure was unbearable.

Moz and Abby, who was now carrying Jack, were ahead of him. Without thinking, Tom lashed out with his heavily booted foot, kicking at a pile of rock and earth. The debris scattered but it wasn't enough. He kicked it again for good measure and felt a shaft of pain in his ankle as a larger rock moved.

Good.

Tom sucked in a breath. It was a tiny vent for the pressure inside but it helped. He paused for a moment to wriggle his foot and check that he hadn't been stupid enough to injure his ankle, and it was in that moment that his headlight caught the shine of something pale in the rubble.

Frowning, he stooped and brushed some more earth away. The pale thing was plastic. The head of a doll. A male doll, who was wearing camouflage clothing.

Action Man? It had to be.

Tom had a grin on his face as he eased himself through the gap that had allowed them access to the mine shaft in the first place.

Mission accomplished.

He brushed some more dirt off the toy and waited a minute or two until Shelley and Moz had moved away from where Abby was sitting with Jack in her arms, a blanket now draped over her shoulders. Shelley was helping Moz go through the backpacks, looking for something for Jack to eat and drink.

Tom walked towards them, holding Action Man behind his back, a little unsure how to present his find.

Good grief…he was feeling *shy*?

He was certainly feeling something that wasn't anger anymore.

Seeing Abby sitting there, holding her son, *their* son, was doing something very odd to that mix of emotion in his gut. Tom could feel his throat closing up. A weird prickle at the back of his eyes.

Tears?

The thought was shocking enough to stop him in his tracks for a moment.

They were safe. His son. The woman he still loved.

There was peace to be found in that realisation. The kind of satisfaction that came with the success of any tough job and then some. Then a whole heap more because he had a real connection to these people.

Tom swallowed hard. He moved again. Got close to Abby and Jack and then crouched down into a squat.

'Guess what I found?'

He'd never forget the way Jack stared at him with those wide, startled eyes. The way his grubby little face lit up with the biggest grin in the world when he saw his beloved toy.

The ordeal was forgotten.

'You okay, buddy?' Tom had to check. 'Nothing hurts?'

Jack shook his head.

'Not scared anymore?'

He shook his head again. He clutched Action Man a bit tighter and then his grin reappeared. A cheeky flash that Tom recognised.

God knew, he'd seen it in photographs often enough. In the mirror, even.

'I *was* scared,' Jack whispered. 'But now I liked it.'

A huff of sound came from Abby and Tom's gaze shifted to capture hers. They both knew exactly what Jack meant. That he might have been terrified at the time but now that it was all over, he wouldn't mind doing it again because the way he felt now made it all worthwhile.

How was it possible to feel such an instant bond with another human being? That simple, childish logic had gone straight to a place in Tom's heart that nobody else had ever touched.

Even Abby. This small child, who'd probably never experienced anything really dangerous because he had such a protective mother, understood exactly why Tom did what he did.

Could he feel that same exhilaration without knowing what it was? Tom could recognise the fizzing sensation running through his veins. He'd experienced it often enough. It was the thrill of still being alive after the adrenaline rush of facing danger had receded.

When you knew you were safe and you could breathe again. When everything about life seemed to have more colour. More meaning. The time when it was so obvious that life was worth living.

Shelley came back with water and muesli bars for Abby and Jack. They all needed to eat and drink something and then they could get moving. It would be a long haul getting back through the bush to where they'd left the helicopter, especially with a small child to carry now. And with Abby's sore knee.

Except maybe they wouldn't have to after all. As the light brightened a notch, Tom could hear something that swiftly became the recognisable chop of an Iroquois helicopter.

They had sent in the troops.

Moz let out a whoop and pumped a fist in Tom's direction. He grinned back. Things were looking up.

And then he looked back to where Abby was now standing with Jack. His son was bouncing up and down, pointing at the approaching helicopter. He held his mum's hand on one side. The pointing hand was still firmly clutching Action Man.

Tom could feel his grin fading.

How come he'd never realised this before?

That it wasn't the absence of danger that gave you that feeling that life was worth living.

It was *this* feeling. The connection with other people. *Love.*

The realisation was shocking. It pretty much contradicted the premise his life had always been built around.

What the hell was he supposed to do about that?

CHAPTER SEVEN

IT WAS SO QUIET.

Everything and everyone on Kaimotu Island seemed to be caught in a stunned silence.

It seemed that the worst was over. They could expect a lot more aftershocks, of course, but none of them would be anywhere near the intensity of that first dreadful quake.

Abby was back at the information centre where the focus was now on looking to the immediate future rather than urgent rescue missions.

Everyone was accounted for. Those unfortunate enough to have been trapped in buildings had been rescued. Anyone who had suffered serious injuries had been airlifted to the mainland. Engineers were swarming over the township, assessing whether it was safe for people to go back to their houses and start cleaning up.

For the first time, Abby spared a thought for her own cottage. Until now, whether her home had survived the quake had been inconsequential compared to Jack's safety. Now all she wanted to do was to take her son and…and go home.

She had never been this exhausted in her life. Too tired to eat, even, despite the fact that the Hayward sisters were providing delicious bacon butties straight off a barbecue for anyone who wanted breakfast. They were fussing over Jack, who sat at one end of the long table, eating bacon with one hand and still clutching his Action Man toy with the other.

Tom was beside him, clearly enjoying his own generously stuffed sandwich, talking with other rescue personnel between bites. There were a lot of people here. Stood down from active duty now because they were all well overdue for a rest and, as far as anybody could tell, nobody was in imminent danger any longer.

The rest of the school children were being taken off the beach below where the bus was stuck. Moz had gone out on the boat so that he could get back to the helicopter and retrieve it. In just a few hours, he and Tom would be expected to take that helicopter back to their Auckland base and step back into their own lives.

What would happen then?

Tom hadn't said anything about where they would go from here.

He hadn't said much of anything at all, really, since they'd all come out of the mine shaft.

And Abby hadn't said anything much to Tom, either, because what she needed to say was so big she had no idea where to start.

He had saved her son. *His* son. Nobody else would have even attempted that dangerous rescue. Apart from herself, of course, but she could never have done it without Tom.

The debt of gratitude was too deep to measure but it came with a mix of fear, as well. What might Tom expect in return? How much was this going to change their lives?

'You okay, Abby?' Mike Henley looked pale with fatigue. 'I heard about what happened up at the mine. He's quite something, isn't he?'

Had Mike noticed that she was standing here by herself, staring at Tom Kendrick? Oh, help… How many other people had noticed?

And he was standing right beside Jack. How long would it take for somebody to notice the physical similarities between Tom and Jack? It was amazing that one of the Hayward sisters hadn't spotted the exciting discovery and said something already, but maybe everybody was just too tired right now.

'I'm okay, thanks, Mike.' Abby tried to sound convincing. 'I just want to get home and see what state the cottage is in. Get some sleep, maybe. Do you know where Ben is? I'd better find out if I'm needed up at the hospital first.'

'What's needed is for you to get some rest,' Mike told her. 'You and Jack. We've got plenty of people holding the fort for the moment. Ben and Ginny are coping up at the hospital. Did you hear that Squid Davies died?'

'Oh…*no*. What happened?'

'The search dogs found him under a pile of cray pots but he seemed to be okay. Had a bump on the head but he wasn't keen on being dragged up to the hospital. Apparently Ben and Ginny fixed him up and left him to have a rest while they went to treat someone else and when they went back, there he was. Dead.'

Abby swallowed back the prickle of tears. 'Ben must be devastated. He and Squid were such good friends.'

'I think Ginny was more upset about it, actually. Ben's saying that we have to remember that Squid *was* ninety-seven years old and he'd had a great life. And he had been having a few problems with his ticker. Ben reckons he died peacefully. People are already saying that he died with a smile on his face and a bubble over his head that read, "I told you so."'

Abby had to smile. It was true. Squid had been forecasting the 'big one' for a while now and nobody had taken any notice. Being proved right was a pretty good note to go out on. Especially when you'd reached the grand old age of ninety-seven.

Would she live that long? Get to see her grandchildren having children, maybe?

Maybe she'd still be living alone in her little cottage. Wandering down to sit on a pile of cray pots and enjoy the sunshine. Remembering Squid and his prophecy of doom.

The prospect was a long way from being appealing.

'I'll get hold of the engineers,' Mike was saying now, 'and see if they've had a look at your place yet. Then I'll organise some transport.'

'We can walk,' Abby protested. 'It's not that far.'

'You're dead on your feet, Abby. You look like you've been run over by a steamroller.'

Abby had to smile. It felt like that, too. Physically and emotionally. Her feet felt like lead as she started moving again.

'You had enough bacon, Jack? It's time we went home.'

'Can Tom come, too?'

'I…uh…' Abby managed to avoid catching Tom's

gaze. He had crashed back into her life and already seemed to have penetrated too far, too fast past its safe boundaries. The home she'd created in the last six years was the only part of her life he hadn't entered. Could she cope with having to share that, as well?

'Tom's got things he has to do,' she told Jack. 'With… with the helicopter and stuff.'

'It'll be a while before Moz gets back.' Tom's voice sounded deceptively calm. 'I'd like to see that you both get home safely.'

'Cool…' Jack grinned up at Tom. 'I can show you my tree hut. I built it all by myself.'

'Did you, now? Didn't Action Man help?'

'Nah… I built it when I was *four*.'

Tom looked suitably impressed. 'I'd like to see that.'

Abby closed her eyes as she took a slow breath. It hadn't taken much building. It wasn't even a tree hut, really. Jack had discovered the hollow centre of the old macrocarpa hedge that ran along the back of their garden and he'd claimed it for his 'hut'. It was his favourite place to play. A place that only special people were invited to visit.

She'd never been allowed to crawl inside. Jack had sawn off some tiny branches to make a hole big enough for her to deliver snacks and drinks but it was *his* space and she respected that.

Now he was inviting Tom to see it. He didn't even know that this man, who'd been a complete stranger until a few hours ago, was his father, but already there was a bond there that she felt excluded from.

And it wasn't a nice feeling. On top of everything

else, it was simply too much to cope with and Abby had the horrible feeling she might burst into tears.

'Abby? We've got a Jeep going your way. Engineers tell me your chimney's come down but the rest of the house is sound. Bit of a mess with broken crockery and stuff, that's all. Will you be okay to start sorting that yourself?'

'She won't be by herself.' It was Tom who spoke. 'I'm going with them. Moz can contact me by radio when he's back. Or you can get hold of me if I'm needed elsewhere.'

'You're on stand-down for now, mate. You've done more than enough.' Mike gripped Tom's shoulder. 'We can't thank you enough. I'm sure Abby feels the same way.' He was smiling at Jack now.

Abby hurriedly scooped her small son into her arms. It would look pretty churlish if she refused Tom's intention to accompany them to see what needed to be sorted out at the cottage. And she was too tired to argue. This was clearly going to happen and somehow, she had to deal with it.

The driver of the Jeep was Ruth's husband, Damien.

'Ruth's at home with the kids now,' he told Abby. 'We got off lightly. Something to be said for living in a train carriage, I guess. Lost some of the pottery in the shed but that's all. I wanted to do something to help the others.'

He had plenty more to tell her about in the short drive.

'There's offers of help pouring in from all over New Zealand. Tradesmen are offering to donate their time to help rebuild things and others are already donating

money to buy the materials. Kind of restores your faith
in human nature, eh?'

'I'm often amazed by the good things that can fall
out of what seems like a horrible package no one would
want to accept.'

Tom's words were quiet. They were in response to
Damien's comment. But his eyes were fixed on the rear-
view mirror and it felt like he was talking only to her.
Funny how reflected eye contact could feel just as intense as the real thing.

Did he mean meeting her again?

No. She ignored the skip her heart took. He meant
finding out about Jack. Learning that he was a father.

It didn't take long to get to Abby's house, a stone's
throw from the beach. Small and old, the weather-
board dwelling had a corrugated iron roof now heavily dented by where the brick chimney had toppled and
come crashing down to leave only a few jagged bricks
at roof level.

'That'll need covering before it rains,' Tom observed.
'Lucky you had an iron roof. Something like tiles and
you would have found that pile of bricks right inside
your house.'

'Mmm.' The agreement was somewhat strangled.
That pile of bricks was a tiny patch of destruction compared to what had happened elsewhere but it was a very
personal patch and Abby had to blink back tears as she
looked at it.

It felt like she had a similar pile of rubble somewhere
deep inside her. The barrier between her life before and
after Jack had come into it?

The safety walls?

* * *

Tom gave himself a mental kick.

What a stupid observation to have made about the chimney. No wonder Abby had made that dismissive sound. Or that she was now walking away from him.

It was more than reluctance to engage in conversation, though, wasn't it?

Abby hadn't wanted him to come here at all. She was reluctant to invite him any further into her life, and fair enough…he got that.

But this was also where Jack lived and surely he had the right to see where his son had been living for the last five years?

Where he'd been cradled and fed as a newborn?

Where he'd taken his first wobbly steps?

Spoken his first word?

Made his first tree hut?

An entire lifetime for Jack so far, and Tom hadn't been remotely aware of any of it. He'd missed out on so much. But if he gave that any more head space, that anger that he'd been so aware of when he'd been stomping his way out of the mine tunnel could resurface. If he didn't want to miss out on a whole lot more of Jack's life, it would be advisable to make sure it didn't.

So Tom allowed himself only a frown. A scowl that was directed squarely at Abby's back as she opened the front door of her cottage. He couldn't maintain the scowl, then, because his eyebrows shot up.

'Your door's unlocked?' Super-safety-conscious Abby didn't even bother making sure her home was secure these days?

'No reason to lock it,' she said. 'Not in the off-season,

anyway. The only time stuff is likely to get stolen is when there are thousands of tourists around.'

'Mmm...' It wasn't lost on Tom that the sound he made was a perfect echo of Abby's reaction to his comment about the chimney but he didn't like the idea of Abby taking safety for granted. For herself or Jack.

Abby ignored his response. Holding Jack's hand, she walked down the short hallway into the space at the back of the cottage—a room that ran the width of the house and contained both a kitchen and living area.

The chimney stack might have fallen outside the house, but bricks and mortar and a lot of dust had also tumbled down what remained of the structure and had billowed out into the room. What looked like dirty icing sugar coated ornaments and pictures that had fallen from the mantelpiece and a heap of books dislodged from shelves.

Chairs had toppled beside an old, scrubbed pine dining table and a light fitting dangled from a wire, well below where it had been attached to the ceiling. It was the kitchen that had suffered the most damage, however. Cupboard doors were open and their contents of crockery and glassware lay in broken piles on the dusty wooden floorboards.

'Careful, Jack,' Abby said. 'Don't walk there.'

'Why not?'

'The broken bits have got sharp edges. I don't want you getting cut.'

Tom found himself nodding agreement. Not just because he didn't want Jack getting injured, either, but because this sounded more like the Abby he knew. The safety-conscious one.

He had learned so many things about this woman in less than a day. He'd learned that she was a fiercely protective mother and that she had more courage than you could shake a stick at and that she was terrified of losing the people she loved because of the way her parents had been ripped out of her life. It was a relief to recognise something he could remember. Like the way she'd always checked that the door was locked. And double-wrapping a broken glass in newspaper so that the person collecting their rubbish wouldn't get cut.

Jack's eyes were wide. 'It's messy,' he announced.

Abby actually smiled. 'It's okay, hon. Mess is something we can fix.'

'Will my tree house be messy, too?'

'I wouldn't think so.'

'Can I go and see?'

'Sure.' Abby lifted Jack over the broken crockery, her own boots crunching through the shards as she carried him to the French doors beyond the dining table.

Tom noticed the garden now. A small area bordered by a thick green hedge. The clothesline was a rope tied to a tree at one end and a branch of the hedge at the other, propped up in the middle by a tall, forked branch of driftwood. There were Jack-sized clothes pegged on the line, along with towels and some very feminine underwear.

Deliberately averting his gaze as soon as he realised it had been snagged, Tom looked at the vegetable patch on the other side of the garden, which was clearly carefully tended. Jack was heading towards the hedge behind the vegetable patch, to one side of the gap cut into the tall hedge to leave an archway effect. The gap was filled by a wooden gate and a view of the beach and sea on the other side.

The sun was climbing higher into the sky now and the sea looked astonishingly blue. The garden had a shady area under the tree the clothesline was attached to and Tom noticed the old tractor tyre that had been filled with sand from the beach. A rather rusty toy digger and some plastic dinosaurs were arranged around the edge. Had Jack played in that when he'd been younger? Maybe while Abby had been tending the vegetable garden?

His voice felt curiously raw when he spoke. 'This is an amazing spot,' he said. 'What a great place for a kid to grow up in.'

Abby turned slowly to meet his gaze but she didn't respond immediately. There was a question in her eyes, as if she was waiting for him to say something more. Something about the disadvantages of growing up without a father, perhaps?

But Tom didn't say anything like that. He held Abby's gaze and then he smiled. 'He's a great kid, Abby. You must be very proud of him.'

She nodded slowly. She smiled but her lips wobbled. She opened her mouth as if she was about to speak but no words came out.

And Tom got that, too. Where could they start? With how he'd recognised himself in Jack so instantly when he'd said, 'I was scared but now I liked it'? With whether they told Jack that he was his father before or after they talked about where they went from here?

'There's an awful lot we need to talk about,' he said into the silence. 'But right now we're both beyond exhausted and we need time, and I think you've got enough on your plate.' He let his gaze sweep the domestic devastation around their feet.

Abby's breath came out in a big whoosh as though she'd been holding it.

'Thanks,' she whispered.

'What can I do to help?'

Abby shook her head. 'I think I need to get some sleep. I'm sure Jack does, too. Then I'll do a bit of tidying up and find out what's happening at work. Whether I'm needed there.'

'Have you got food in the house? Is your water working?'

'I'll check.' Abby's feet crunched again as she moved to the kitchen bench. She turned on the tap and nodded. 'It looks fine.'

'Power?'

'I've got a generator in the shed.'

'Let's check that.'

The generator appeared to be undamaged. Abby started to walk back to the house in front of Tom but then stopped and turned to face him.

'Tom…I haven't said thank you. Not properly. I…I don't know how…'

Her eyes looked huge. And were such a dark blue that Tom knew these words were coming straight from her heart. He had to swallow around the lump in his throat.

'There's no need,' he said gruffly.

'There is.' He could see the muscles move in Abby's throat as she swallowed hard. 'I know how dangerous it was to rescue Jack and I know that if it hadn't been you there, it probably wouldn't have happened, and…

and I just want you to know how much that means to me. Jack's…he's my whole life…'

'It was you that rescued him, Abby.'

'I couldn't have done it by myself.' Abby gave a huge sniff and offered him a wry smile. 'And you know something else?'

'What?'

'I think I kind of get why you do what you do, now. It's pretty amazing, doing something that dangerous and saving a life.'

'Mmm…' Tom couldn't identify the emotion welling up inside him. Pride that Abby respected what he did for a living? Or was it relief that they were connecting on this level?

Hope for something he couldn't define yet? Some kind of future?

'It's kind of like a drug, isn't it? That feeling when you know you've succeeded?'

'Yeah…it is.'

'I wonder if that's how my parents felt when they'd conquered a mountain. If they got addicted to that adrenaline rush and the euphoria that would have come after it when they knew they'd survived.'

Tom opened his mouth. He wanted to tell Abby that she might have learned what drove him, but this experience had taught him something much bigger. That what was important in life wasn't the adrenaline rush or the euphoria but the connection between people. The kind of connection he'd felt when he'd seen Abby holding Jack outside the mine.

He'd just experienced an echo of that extraordinarily

powerful feeling when Abby had been telling him she understood why his job was so important to him.

But he couldn't tell her any of that. Because she might push him away? Yes. The risk was too big to take because he'd not only lose her this time, he'd lose Jack as well.

But he had to say something.

'They got it wrong,' he said softly. 'You didn't just lose your parents. They lost you. And they'll never meet their grandchild.'

Abby blinked, her eyes going misty as she absorbed his words. For just a moment they were caught and Tom knew she understood that he was trying to tell her how much *he* cared.

And it felt...like the pieces of something broken were fitting themselves back together. As if a magic spell had been cast and Abby would open her mouth and say something that would provide the glue to hold those pieces in place.

She did open her mouth.

'Tom...I...'

'Tom...' Jack's face appeared through the branches of the hedge. 'Come and see. It's not messy in here.'

'I'm coming, buddy.' But Tom couldn't move just yet. He searched Abby's face and held his breath, waiting for her to finish whatever it was she'd been about to say.

But the spell had been broken. A second ticked past, feeling like much, much longer. And then another one.

And then Jack was right beside them, impatient to show Tom his tree house. Tugging on his hand.

'Come and see,' he implored. 'You *promised*.'

Tom was too big to crawl right inside the small space

but he could fit in far enough to admire the dim cavern created by the twisted trunks and branches overhead and the carpet of long-dead needle leaves on the ground. There were more plastic dinosaurs in here. A tiny, wooden child's chair. And a shoebox.

'That's Action Man's bed,' Jack told him. 'For when he's tired.'

'I'll bet he's tired now after the big adventure you guys have just had.'

'Mmm.' Jack's face twisted into a gigantic yawn at the mere mention of being tired.

'Might be time that you and Action Man and Mum all had a bit of a nap in the house. Shall we go and see what Mum's doing?'

'Okay.' Jack wriggled back out of his cubby hole. He still had Action Man clutched in his hand. 'He wasn't scared, you know. When he got buried in the mine.'

'Not even a little bit?'

Jack thought about this. 'Maybe a little bit,' he admitted. His big brown eyes were worried, though. Was he admitting some kind of failure?

Tom bent down so he could talk very quietly. Man to man.

'It's okay to be scared, Jack. Everybody gets scared sometimes.'

'Even if you're brave?'

'Especially when you're brave. You can only *be* brave if you get scared.'

Jack was frowning hard. Trying to understand.

'If you're not scared then there's nothing you need to be brave about, is there?'

'No-o-o…' Jack bit his lip but then his face lit up.

He understood. He took a deep breath. 'I was really, really scared,' he whispered. 'When I was all by myself in the big hole.'

Tom nodded solemnly. 'That's how I know that you're really, really brave.'

Jack's little chest puffed out with pride but his face was very serious. 'Were *you* scared, too?'

'Oh, yeah...'

Jack nodded, satisfied. And then he nodded again as if coming to a decision. 'We won't tell Mummy we were scared, eh?'

'Nah...I reckon it can be our secret.'

This time they shared a smile. And then they started walking back to the house.

'I could tell you another secret,' Jack offered.

'What's that?'

'Well, Nathan at school's got a tree house, too, only his is really in a tree. You have to climb a ladder to get into it. He says he built it all by himself but it's not true. His dad built it.'

'Dads like doing that kind of stuff. And Nathan might have helped a lot.'

'I guess.' Jack was silent for a moment. They had reached the French doors of the cottage by the time he spoke again. 'I haven't got a dad,' he said.

Abby was picking up pieces of broken glass and putting them into a cardboard box. The piece she was holding dropped with a clatter as she heard Jack's words and then she froze, crouched on the floor in front of them.

'I'd really *like* to have one,' Jack continued. His tone was light. Conversational almost. He was looking up at Tom. 'D'ya think *you* could maybe be my dad?'

Oh, man… Here it was, being offered to him as if it would be the easiest thing in the world to step into his son's life. Except, of course, it wouldn't be.

Abby shot to her feet. There was a look of utter panic in her face as she turned.

'Tom lives in Auckland, Jack. It's a long way away from here.'

Something huge welled up inside Tom at the prospect of being dismissed like this, but he kept his tone as light as Jack's had been.

'It's not that far.'

'Far enough.' Abby's words sounded choked. She was staring at him. Warning him not to go any further down this track. Not yet.

Maybe not ever?

They *were* too far apart for this but it had nothing to do with the physical distance between their homes. That factor paled into insignificance compared to what Abby was really talking about—the emotional distance between them.

For now, Tom knew he had no choice. He had to respect that. Even if it was killing him.

Abby was still staring at him in horror.

Jack was staring at him, too, looking hopeful.

Tom was spared having to find an answer for either of them by his radio crackling into life.

'Tank? You there, mate? Do you read?'

He unclipped the radio and pressed the button. 'Loud and clear, Moz. What's up?'

'We're good to go. Someone's on the way to collect you and bring you up to the helipad. Should be a vehicle just about there.'

Sure enough, a car's horn could be heard tooting outside.

'Roger that,' Tom said. 'On my way.'

He reattached his radio. Jack was looking impressed. He'd totally forgotten the question he'd asked and Tom wasn't about to remind him.

'I've got to go, buddy.' He ruffled Jack's hair. 'But I'll see you soon, okay?'

Abby followed him out of the front door and down the path. 'Why did you say that? He'll be asking me every day now, waiting for you to come back.'

Tom stopped walking just before he reached the waiting vehicle and turned to face Abby. It was important that she heard every word.

'I said it because it's true. I *will* be back. As soon as I can arrange something.'

Abby sucked in a breath but he didn't give her time to say anything.

'I intend to be part of Jack's life from now on,' he told her. 'I'm not sure how it's going to work but there's no way I'm walking away from my son.'

Or you, he wanted to add. *Not this time.*

He managed to hold those words back. Abby had enough to process in coming to terms with the fact that her son now had a father in his life.

'Bye, Abby.' The urge to reach out and pull Abby close was overwhelming. Almost as great as it had been when he'd pulled her through the gap in the sinkhole. But it wasn't the same. She and Jack were both safe, now. In their own home. There was no reason to pull her close and hold her tight. To wish for even an accidental kiss.

He couldn't even hug her like a good friend saying goodbye. The depth of emotion she was clearly coping with herself, judging by the darkness of her eyes and the tight way her lips were pressed together, was screaming a warning that it would not be a good idea.

He had to touch her, though. It was just his hand that he reached out. Just his thumb that he used to brush her cheek with a feather-like stroke.

'I'll be in touch,' he promised.

And then he had to get into the vehicle and be driven away from the beach-side cottage. In a very short space of time he would be in a helicopter, being flown away from Kaimotu Island.

He'd never been here before. He'd been here for less than a full day.

How on earth could it feel like this?

Like he was ripping out his heart and leaving it behind?

CHAPTER EIGHT

THE FUNERAL FOR Squid Davies was held three days after the big quake, and the small chapel was stuffed to the gills and overflowing outside with almost every adult islander. Everybody had loved Squid—the indomitable old fisherman who had been an island icon for as long as anybody could remember.

Abby was sitting in a back pew beside Ben's father, Doug McMahon. Ailsa sat on his other side and she had Ginny beside her. Ginny had her eyes fixed on Ben as he moved to the front of the chapel to give the eulogy. Ben was still using a cane to help him walk, thanks to the injuries he'd suffered only a week ago after rescuing Henry from under a piano. He was only just out of hospital and he looked very pale.

The look on Ginny's face advertised something more than concern for his physical wellbeing, however. There was something on the young doctor's face that struck a very poignant chord with Abby.

She loves him, she thought. So much that she can't imagine her life without Ben in it.

Abby knew what that kind of love was like. How it could make your life unbelievably wonderful. How it could come so close to destroying it when things went wrong.

Like they'd gone wrong for her and Tom.

'Squid asked me to speak today, and everyone here knows Squid,' Ben began. 'He liked to predict what happens so he made sure he wrote this before the earthquake, just in case, telling me what to say.'

A ripple of laughter echoed in the space but Abby didn't join in.

She wished someone was around to predict what was going to happen for her.

Tom was coming back.

And the prospect was deeply disturbing.

For the last few days Abby had been doing what everybody on the island was doing right now: trying to get her life back to some semblance of normality. Thinking about Tom coming back made it seem impossible. Nothing was ever going to be 'normal' again.

Ben's quiet words from Squid about his health issues and how nobody had listened to his predictions flowed over her head. He absolved everyone from blame in the end, saying that nobody really knew anything, you could only guess about what the future held.

Despite Abby's penchant for guessing the worst possible scenarios, somewhere between Squid's funeral and school reopening a few days later, she realised that thinking about Tom coming back was giving her a small thrill every time it happened. A curl of sensation that flickered somewhere deep in her belly.

She recognised that sensation. From way back, when she'd first noticed Tom in his rescue overalls, delivering a critically ill patient to the emergency department in which she'd been working. It had begun to happen whenever she'd heard the swishing sound of the automatic doors to the ambulance bay opening. Or caught a flash of red clothing amongst the emergency services personnel. It had been the thrill of anticipation laced with attraction.

Desire, laced with hope.

In some form, Tom intended to come back into her life. Did it matter that he was only coming back because of Jack?

Well…yes and no.

No, because otherwise he might not have chosen to come back at all.

But yes, because Abby would never know if he might have wanted to see her again if Jack didn't exist.

Abby knew perfectly well she could be setting herself up for renewed heartbreak if she allowed hope to bloom. And what if they *did* rekindle something? Just because she had new insight into the extraordinary satisfaction that could come from putting your own life on the line to save another, it didn't mean that she was prepared to let her son risk the devastation that could come from loving a father who had that kind of addiction.

But any choice in the matter had been taken out of her hands the moment she'd confirmed Jack's paternity, hadn't it? She couldn't protect Jack now. He had the right to know who his father was and to have a relationship with him. Tom had had those rights for even longer and Abby knew she'd been wrong in keeping her secret. Tom had every right to be furious with her.

Maybe that was why she hadn't heard from him yet.

Was he consulting a solicitor, maybe? Asking about his entitlements as a father? About potential custody of his son, even?

Oh…God… She was doing it again. Dreaming up the worst possible scenario. Messing with her own head by dredging up the past or worrying about the future so much she lost sight of the good things that were happening in the present.

And, despite the huge trauma of the earthquake, the grief over people who had lost their lives and the enormous inconvenience of trying to work around services and supplies that were broken or missing, there *were* good things happening.

Ben and Ginny, for one.

The confusion and longing she'd seen in Ginny's face at Squid's funeral had been replaced by a glow of pure joy. She and Ben were engaged now, planning a wedding, as soon as things got a little closer to being normal around here, and a future that would see them living and working together as an integral part of a community of which they were both an important part.

Abby might have come here as a stranger but she felt part of it now, too. She was as happy as everybody else about the news. And she was a part of something much bigger, too. Something that was making her feel like a 'real' islander.

The community of Kaimotu Island had always been tight knit but there was a new and powerful bond forming in the wake of the disaster. People whose houses had been damaged more than others were taken into the houses of neighbours or friends while repairs were done. The cabins in the camping grounds were all occupied.

People whose businesses had been closed because of damage to the town centre were offered new premises, some of them in caravans, and the local men who were part of civil defence used their status to go into places deemed off limits to the general population to retrieve stock and whatever else was needed to make a start in getting businesses and trades operating again.

Heavy machinery had arrived by vehicle ferries and there were diggers and cranes all over the place. Supplies of timber and roofing materials were stacked in huge piles near the jetty. Owners of bed-and-breakfast establishments and motels had opened their doors to volunteers willing to come from the mainland and share their expertise and labouring skills. There were builders and engineers, electricians and plumbers. Counsellors, even, who wanted to help people deal with the trauma. And there were others, who just wanted to offer their time and muscles.

One of them was Tom.

He just turned up at the hospital one day, about ten days after he'd left. Abby was in the clinic's reception area, chatting to Ben's sister Hannah. The afternoon clinic wasn't due to start for an hour and there were no emergencies on the way in that they knew about so they both turned to see who was coming unexpectedly through the door.

They both instantly forgot whatever it was they were talking about and simply stared as Tom walked towards them. He was grinning at Hannah.

'Hi, there.'

'Hi.'

Hannah sounded a bit breathless. Impressed, even though Tom obviously hadn't come by helicopter and he wasn't wearing his rescue service overalls or anything else that advertised his profession as an elite paramedic. This was just Tom, in faded blue jeans and a black T-shirt, with a bag slung over his shoulder, but to Abby, he'd never looked better. Or more important. Abby was more than a bit breathless herself. Maybe she'd forgotten *how* to breathe.

He'd come back.

Whatever this new chapter in her life held, it was about to begin. Abby's mouth felt dry and she noticed that Tom's grin faded as he turned his gaze from Hannah to meet her gaze.

'Hey, Abby...I'm back.'

Stupidly, all she could do was nod. This was huge. Scary but...exciting, too.

'I've taken a couple of weeks' leave,' he told her. 'I offered my services to come and help with the clean-up. There's a briefing for the group I came with this afternoon but I wanted to come and say hi first.'

Abby nodded again. A smile wanted to emerge but her lips wouldn't cooperate. 'Hi,' she managed.

Hannah was still staring. 'You're one of the air-rescue guys, aren't you? You came here when the earthquake first happened. You took Abby away with you.'

'I sure did. I needed her.' Tom was smiling at Hannah again. He flicked a glance back at Abby but she couldn't read it. Had he ever *really* needed her?

'And you rescued Jack out of the mine. Everybody was talking about that.'

'Were they?' Another glance came Abby's way but this time the raised eyebrow made it easy to read. What else had everybody been talking about? The physical similarity between him and Abby's fatherless son, perhaps?

Abby took a deep breath. 'Hannah, this is Tom Kendrick. He's...he's an old friend from when I used to live in Auckland.'

'Ohhh...' Hannah was a teenager. She was primed to read between the lines and pick up on any potentially romantic nuances. Her smile revealed the conclusion she had come to. The glance she gave Abby was impressed. Then she smiled at Tom.

'Where are you staying? In the camping ground?'

'Not sure yet.' The glance Abby got this time was lightning fast. Almost embarrassed?

Hannah hadn't missed it. Her smile widened. 'Nothing wrong with a couch,' she offered.

'Hannah!' Abby's jaw dropped. Having Tom here on the island again was one thing. Having him staying in her small cottage would be something else entirely. She tried to shake off the intense shaft of *that* sensation in her belly and found she was actually shaking her head. 'How 'bout you go and check if there's a clean sheet on the bed in the consult room?'

Left alone with Tom, Abby didn't know quite what to say. She fiddled with the papers on the reception desk, putting the list of the outpatient appointments on the top. There were a lot of them, as many islanders continued to recover from minor to moderate injuries sustained in the quake. She could feel the steady impact of Tom's gaze, however, and had to raise her eyes.

'I want to get to know Jack,' Tom said quietly. 'And I want him to know that I'm his father.'

Abby nodded. Swallowed hard. 'I want that, too.'

'I'll probably be quite busy during the days with the working party.'

Abby nodded again. It wouldn't leave that much time to spend with Jack, would it? She took a very deep breath.

'The couch isn't that big,' she said, 'but…if you want to stay…'

The silence seemed to tick on. And on…. Abby couldn't look away from Tom. Did she want this? To have him in her house when she woke up in the mornings? To have time with him in the evenings after Jack was sound asleep?

Oh, yes…

This was for Jack, she reminded herself desperately. This wasn't about Tom wanting time alone with her.

But the look in Tom's eyes suggested that could be part of it.

His nod was decisive. 'I'd better get to the briefing,' he said. He hefted his bag and turned to leave but then looked back. And smiled. 'Thanks, Abby.'

The agonising over what Abby might be thinking about how and when to tell Jack he had a father turned out to be one of those bridges that hadn't needed crossing.

It just happened. On the very first evening when Tom turned up with his bag and Abby casually told Jack that

Tom was going to be staying for a bit to help people fix up their houses.

Jack's nod was solemn.

'Are you going to be my dad while you're here?' He made it sound like it was no big deal.

Tom had trouble making more than a vaguely non-committal sound as he met Abby's gaze over the top of their son's head. He knew his face would be asking a very big question but he wanted to convey reassurance as well.

He fully expected to see a flash of fear in Abby's eyes and he wasn't going to rush this if she wasn't ready.

But, amazingly, what he could see was something soft. And warm.

'Um...' Abby had to clear her throat. 'Not just for while he's here, Jack. Tom's going to be your dad...well, for ever. He...he always has been.'

Jack's eyes seemed to fill half his face and his mouth was an O of amazement. Tom dropped to his haunches so that he was on the same level as this small, aston-ished person.

'I didn't know about you before,' he said carefully. 'But I'm here now.'

'Why didn't you know about me? *I've* always been here.'

Something poignant twisted inside Tom at the child-ish logic. He had no idea how to answer the question and he didn't have to look up to sense Abby's tension. Or know that she was feeling guilty. She was responsible for Jack spending his first five years without a father. For him not knowing he had a son.

Tom expected to feel the heat of the anger that had

been swirling within touching distance ever since he'd found out. Oddly, though, it didn't seem to be there right now. He'd come here knowing he was taking a big step into a new future. A whole new path, even. And it was the future that mattered, not the past. No…it was right now that really mattered.

If this was going to work—this 'being parents' stuff—he and Abby needed to support each other.

Besides, it was easy to step away from something that would hurt Abby. You didn't do things that you knew would hurt someone you loved.

Maybe Abby didn't have any reason to think that he had anything worthwhile to offer her after the way he'd pushed her out of his life years ago, but right now he had the opportunity to make a new beginning.

'It happens,' he told Jack quietly. 'Sometimes people are friends. Even really, really good friends and things happen that makes them think they don't want to be friends anymore.'

Jack was nodding. 'Like me and Nathan. When he wouldn't let me climb up the ladder and go in his tree house. I *cried*.'

It was Tom's turn to nod his understanding. But that twisting thing was happening inside again and he had to swallow to get rid of the tight sensation in his throat. Had Abby cried after he'd pushed her away? When he'd told her it wasn't going to work? That his career was what he lived for and he couldn't be with someone who was going to clip his wings and hold him back?

'But you and Nathan are friends again now?'

'Yes. I'm going to his birthday party next week. We're going to *sleep* in the tree house.'

'I'm not sure about that, hon.' Abby touched Jack's head. 'You'll have the party in the tree house but you might have to sleep in the real house.'

'Why?'

'Well, what if you needed to go to the toilet in the middle of the night? You might forget where you are and fall down the ladder.'

'I wouldn't forget, Mummy. That's silly. I'd remember cos I'd be there and I'd *see* the ladder.'

'You might be really sleepy and think you were dreaming.'

Tom could easily think *he* was dreaming right now. He could feel Jack's small hand on his knee as the little boy edged closer. With Abby's fingers still resting on that silky, dark head, they were all connected.

A…family?

'Can I call you "Dad"?'

The need to know the reason why Tom had been absent in his life up till now seemed to have been forgotten. Or maybe it had simply been deemed unimportant.

Tom tried to smile but his lips wouldn't quite cooperate. 'If that's okay with Mummy, it's fine with me.'

He had to close his eyes for a heartbeat because that stupid word made him wince. Fine? Tom had no idea what it was going to be like having someone call him 'Dad', but he did know it was far too huge to be encompassed by that little word.

He could still feel the touch of Jack's hand on his knee as he crouched here on the floor of Abby's living room. He could feel the connection right through to Abby and he knew that she still had her hand on his head. The feeling of connection strengthened as he heard her soft words.

'It's who you are, Tom. Of course it's okay with me.'

Tom opened his eyes to find Jack staring at him. Then the small boy twisted his neck to look up at his mother.

'Are you and Dad friends again now? Like me and Nathan?'

The tiny silence seemed huge. Filled with how easily the title of fatherhood had fallen from Jack's lips. His acceptance had been instant. Unquestioned. But how was Abby feeling? Tom could feel the thump of his heart as he waited for Abby to answer.

'Yes.' Abby's gaze shifted from Jack to Tom. 'I think so.'

Her eyes were dark enough to show strong feelings. As strong as what was stealing *his* breath away? Did she think that there was a possibility of more than friendship?

Did she *want* that?

'I think so, too,' Tom said, amazed at how calm he sounded. At the smile he managed, while still holding Abby's gaze. She was the one to break the connection, first looking away from Tom and then ruffling Jack's hair before lifting her hand.

And then she turned away.

She had to find something to do with her hands. Something that didn't require any brain power because whatever she had between her ears had turned into some kind of mush. Just as well, the dinner dishes were still piled up on the kitchen bench and it was only a step or two away. Behind her, she could sense Tom getting to his feet. She could hear Jack bouncing.

'Come and see *my* room. I've got books and trucks and…and a helicopter just like yours…'

The voices faded and Abby was left trying to find something solid in the mush of her thoughts.

Hearing her son call Tom 'Dad' like that. As though a missing piece of his life had simply been slotted into where it belonged.

As if they were a real family.

The way Tom had looked at her when she'd said that she thought they were friends again. As if there was something much, much bigger than friendship on offer.

Just the sheer, overwhelming presence of him in her home hunched down like that, with those faded jeans emphasising the muscles in his thighs and that soft, old T-shirt clinging to the equally impressive outline of his shoulders and chest. He could have remained standing and commanded a physical control of this space with no effort at all. He could have taken emotional control, too, and simply told Jack what he needed to be told.

But he hadn't. He'd handed that control to her and his eyes had told her that whatever *she* wanted was okay. He would back her up if she wasn't ready for this. It had been *her* call.

And it had been easy to know what to say. Even when her approval had been sought about whether it was all right for Jack to call him 'Dad'.

Dad. Daddy. The word held such power because it took Abby straight back to her own childhood. To when she'd had a 'real' family and life had seemed perfect. And even after so many years, the pain of missing her parents could sneak up and hit her like a sledgehammer and bring tears to her eyes. A painful lump to her throat.

On top of feeling like, somehow, a real family had been born again just now. When she'd been looking down at Tom, keeping her hand on Jack's head as if that would somehow steady her and remind her that he was hers and always would be. When she'd probably seen too much in that dark gaze of Tom's.

He was here for his son, not to be with his son's mother. Somehow, she had to remember that.

With the last of the pots on the draining-board, Abby wiped her hands on a tea towel and straightened her back, then walked out of the kitchen.

'Jack? It's time to get your pyjamas on and clean your teeth, ready for bed.' She poked her head through the doorway. 'It's a school day tomorrow.'

Oh, help. Tom was sitting on the end of Jack's bed. Half lying, in fact, propped up on one elbow. Jack was lying on his stomach and their heads were almost touching, bent over the glossy pictures of a book about dinosaurs. They both looked up at the same time and if her heart had been wrenched any more, it would have torn into little pieces.

They were *so* alike.

And she loved them. *Both* of them.

If she didn't get some protective barriers up there was no way she was going to cope with having Tom here, getting to know his son.

Keep busy, she ordered herself. Focus on Jack. On work. On the house. Whatever it takes. In a couple of weeks, Tom would be going back to his own life. To the career that meant more to him than anything or anyone else. She had to keep her distance because there was no way she could stand the heartbreak of losing him for a second time.

'I'll find some bedding,' she added, turning away, 'and make up the couch for you, Tom. You've probably got an early start tomorrow.'

How could time be passing so fast?

The days were full-on, with early starts and late finishes. The bonus of volunteer labour was being well used and Tom was happy to be in the thick of it. There were roofs to be patched and made weatherproof after chimneys had fallen, and mounds of bricks and rubble to get shifted. Damaged septic tanks were being replaced and there was a lot of digging that had to be done by hand in awkward places.

Hefty framing was going up around heritage buildings that could be saved but which needed to be protected from further aftershocks in the meantime.

Many of the people Tom was working with were also volunteers from the mainland. He even knew a few of them, including a trio of firemen from Auckland that he'd met at more than one major accident scene. He didn't join them for a few beers after the manual labour was finished for the day, though. While he was enjoying being part of the recovery process, it hadn't been the primary reason for this visit to Kaimotu Island.

The other volunteers had no idea of the real reason he'd come back so soon but there were a lot of locals in and around the working parties and it only took a day or two before Tom realised he was getting some significant looks along with friendly slaps on the back here and there that other volunteers didn't seem to be given.

How could he have forgotten how small communities worked? He might have stayed in blissful ignorance a little longer, too, except that a Jeep slowed and then stopped just in front of him on a morning when he was headed into a site on the main street. A route that Ben McMahon was taking to get up the hill to the hospital.

Ben got out of the Jeep and leaned on the door as he waited for Tom to catch up. 'Hey, Tom... Haven't seen you for a few days and I've been wanting to say hi. How's it going?'

'Great. I think we're beginning to see a bit of progress. Still a lot to be done, of course.'

'It's people like you that are going to make it happen faster. We're all very grateful.'

Tom shrugged off the praise. 'How's it going up at the hospital? I heard you've had to evacuate a ward after they found some cracks.'

'Safety precaution. It's probably only cosmetic but there's a team of engineers coming to give it a thorough inspection today.'

'Abby says you're pretty stretched for manpower still. It's great news that Ginny's going to come on board.'

Ben's grin lit up his face. 'Sure is. I'm the luckiest man alive.'

Tom grinned back. Everybody knew that there was a wedding in the near future for Ben and Ginny. That Button was going to have a real family. An amazing family, from what Tom had been hearing. The kind that cemented communities like this together in the best possible way. Ben's parents were astonishing in their capacity to care for so many people. It was always a highlight of Jack's day when he got to go to the McMahon homestead after school to be looked after by Hannah.

He was wearing Abby down at the moment, begging for one of the kittens that Ailsa was caring for. Button had a black one with a white nose, apparently. Jack wanted the one that had odd black and white splotches all over it. He had already named it Checkers.

'And I'm not the only one with great news,' Ben added. 'I think Jack's the happiest little boy alive right now.'

'He's got the kitten?'

'What? No, I don't know anything about a kitten. I'm talking about him not only having a dad but having one that everybody knows is a real hero.'

'Ohh…' Tom was embarrassed. 'He told you?'

'Actually, it was Button who told us, but I think he's told everybody else. It was news at school the day after you got here.'

Tom's embarrassment deepened. This was pretty personal stuff to have broadcast. And what would people think? That he hadn't wanted to have anything to do with his son until now?

'I didn't know,' he said quietly. 'I probably never would have known if the earthquake hadn't brought me here.'

Ben nodded. 'Abby made that very clear. That she hadn't told you she was pregnant. That it wasn't your fault.'

Tom winced. 'I wouldn't go quite that far. It was my fault that the relationship didn't work out.'

There was a genuine sympathy in Ben's gaze and

his eyebrows had an encouraging lift but he didn't say anything. Maybe his own current state of bliss made him want things to work out for everybody. And he knew Abby, didn't he? He had to know what an amazing person she was. But he didn't know *him* that well and they were blokes, for heaven's sake. Neither of them would be remotely comfortable getting onto emotional territory. Besides, they both had important jobs to get on with.

'I'm working on that.' Tom managed a grin.

Ben's face lit up again and Tom got another one of those friendly back slaps. 'Good luck. And consider yourself invited to the wedding, if you can make it.'

'The reception's going to be a beach party,' Abby told Tom later that night, when he mentioned meeting Ben and getting an invitation to the wedding. 'And I've had a sneak preview of what the wedding dress is going to be like. Ginny will look stunning.'

'I'm sure she will.' Tom's smile looked a bit strained and Abby wasn't surprised. Men like Tom weren't into the whole marriage thing, were they? It was the kind of anchor that heroes functioned better without.

Hmm. Awkward. And Jack wasn't even around to defuse this sudden atmosphere by launching yet another campaign that would result in him getting his own kitten. That morning's attempt had been a portrait of Checkers that was now held in place by magnets on the front of the fridge. He wouldn't be bursting into the room any time soon, either, because this was the sleep-over night for Nathan's birthday party.

It was, in fact, the first night that Abby and Tom had been alone together in the cottage.

Oh…help. Awkwardness had just gained an edge of real tension.

As if she wasn't totally aware of Tom all the time, anyway. Having him sitting to eat with them at the table or crowding the small kitchen to wash up afterwards. Seeing him come out of the bathroom after a shower with his hair in spikes and his chest still bare, or, worse, when he passed close enough for her to smell the clean dampness of his skin. To feel its heat.

Having Jack always there had made it easy to fight the awareness. And the desire that licked at its heels. Until it was safe to go there when she was in her own bed, wrapped in the privacy of darkness.

How was she going to distract herself now? Keep herself safe?

The meal was over. The dishes were done. The little house was very quiet without Jack. Abby could hear the wash of the nearby waves and the forlorn cry of a seagull.

She could wash her coffee mug, at least. Pushing her chair back, Abby got to her feet. 'It'll be a real island do,' she said a little too brightly. 'Something happy everybody can look forward to. You should come…' Oh, Lord, why had she said that? 'I guess you won't still be here, though…'

Tom had got to his feet, as well. He was following her with his own empty mug. 'Would you like me to still be here, Abby?'

'I…' Abby shook off a wave of longing. Her next words came out more harshly than she'd intended.

'What's the point in even asking, Tom? There's nothing here for *you*.'

Tom's mug went down onto the bench with a loud thud. 'What's that supposed to mean? Do you think the fact that I've got a son means *nothing* to me? That *you* mean *nothing*?'

'N-no...' Abby gulped. She meant something to him? What, exactly? 'I was talking about your career. What's most important to you. You couldn't live here.'

Tom took a step closer. 'But you and Jack could come and live in Auckland.' He was speaking more quietly now. With an intensity that revealed this wasn't the first time he'd thought about this. 'We could be a family, Abby. We could...we could get married.'

It was that tiny hesitation that broke Abby's heart. That...*reluctance*. Or an acceptance of the inevitable? He would be marrying her only for Jack's sake. To make them a family.

The result might be something Abby had dreamed of countless times but the means of getting there was not enough. Not nearly enough. She shook her head with a sharpness that spoke of despair.

'Kaimotu's our home,' she said. 'We're happy here.' Up until a few weeks ago she would have automatically added, *We're safe here.* They still were, emotionally.

Or were they? Jack already adored his father and she...well, any safety barriers she'd had around her heart had been showing cracks ever since Tom had shown up so unexpectedly in her life again. And those cracks were widening as she stood here in the silence. Tom seemed to be waiting for her to say something more.

'What makes you think it could possibly work?' she

whispered. Okay, maybe the sexual tension had been there on both sides but he hadn't even tried to kiss her, even though they'd been living in the same house. Jack's house. 'It didn't before.'

'We were good together.'

Abby's breath huffed out in an incredulous snort. 'Good? You told me I was holding you back. Clipping your wings. How does that suddenly become *good*?'

'It's different now.'

'Because of Jack?'

'No.' Tom was still standing very close. His eyes were fixed on Abby's. 'I was wrong. I didn't understand.'

'Understand what?'

'What happened to you when you were just a kid. When you lost your mum and dad.'

Abby huffed again. It was almost a sob. 'And how exactly does that make a difference?'

'If you understand *why* someone feels the way they do, you can work around it. Find a way through.'

When had she wrapped her arms around herself like this? She hadn't even noticed but now she was holding herself tightly, as if she needed comfort.

What was going on here? Why was she feeling so devastated? This was what she wanted, wasn't it? For her and Tom to be together again? So why was she arguing? Trying to push him away?

Because nothing had really changed. If they were together, she would still have to live with that fear of losing him, even if Tom thought he could 'work around it'.

But...she understood, too, now, didn't she? What

drove him? She'd felt it herself, when they'd rescued Jack. She'd told him she understood.

No wonder he was looking bewildered. As confused as she was feeling. She screwed her eyes shut tightly, trying to sort out the whirl of conflicting thoughts.

She could feel Tom moving closer.

She felt his breath on her skin. The touch of the pad of his thumb on her lips that made them part instantly in a response that had become hard wired years ago and simply couldn't be overridden. The soft touch continued to trace her bottom lip and Abby couldn't fight the wave of sensation that rocked her all the way to her toes.

She felt her head tipping back. This track was well worn into her cell memory, too. In a heartbeat it would be Tom's lips instead of his thumb touching hers and… *yes*…he would slide his fingers into her hair like that— the press of his fingertips as arousing as the magic he could make with his lips and tongue.

The desire Abby had been fighting ever since she'd first laid eyes on Tom again became incandescent. The heat was obviously contagious because Tom stripped off his T-shirt moments later and then helped Abby shed hers. The garments puddled on the floor beside them and then there was a moment's absolute stillness as they stood there, simply looking at each other.

Abby drank in the sight of him. He was the most beautiful man she had ever seen. All that glorious, olive skin covering sheer masculine power. The irresistibly vulnerable copper discs of his nipples and the invitation of that soft arrow of dark hair that dragged her gaze down to where the denim of his jeans cut low across the ridges of a totally ripped abdomen.

Her fingers itched to release the button on those jeans. To hear the delicious slide of the zip opening. She knew what she would find and…dear Lord…she'd never wanted anything this much.

But Abby dragged her gaze up because she could feel the touch of Tom's gaze warming the soft swell of her breasts as they pushed against the lacy cups of her bra. She could sense that his fingers were itching, too. To reach behind her and unfasten the clasp of that small undergarment.

But as she looked up, so did Tom. No wonder it's called 'eye contact', Abby realised. The touch wasn't physical and yet this was the most powerful grip in which she had ever felt herself held.

The touch of souls rather than bodies.

Abby felt as though some force was lifting her. As though her feet were no longer touching the floor, and she recognised this feeling as easily as her skin cells remembered Tom's touch.

This was love.

For both of them.

Could they make it work? *Really* work this time?

Impossible to think into the future right now. Abby's ability to leap ahead and think of everything that could possibly make something *not* work failed her completely this time. She couldn't think a week ahead. Or even a day.

Ten seconds was about all she could manage. No, less than that. Just as long as it took her to stand on tip-toe and lean forward so that she would feel the press of Tom's bare skin against her breasts. To wind her arms around his neck and pull him in for the kiss that would take them straight to her bed.

The future could wait.

Thinking could wait.

All Abby wanted to do was to sink into this astonishing explosion of sensation. Pure bliss.

All she wanted was Tom.

CHAPTER NINE

BLISS HUNG AROUND.

Somewhere very close to the surface of your skin, Abby decided. The memory might not be as intense as the real thing but it was still magic. It sparked little curls of something delicious deep in her belly, and made her feel as if her bones had softened. And she knew it made her smile because Jack noticed sometimes.

'Why are you smiling, Mummy?' he'd ask.

'Because I'm happy,' she would tell him. 'Because I love you so much.'

And that would send little Jack on his way. Before his busy day could be interrupted by one of those annoying squeezy hugs.

It didn't take much to scratch the surface and release a little bit of that bliss, either. Just the sound of her phone indicating a text message could do it these days because it was usually Tom. He'd be asking about what Jack had been up to that day or how work was going for Abby and he'd sign himself 'T' with an 'x' for a kiss.

The sight of a particularly dark head of wavy hair or some other physical similarity that reminded her of Tom could lift that release catch, too. Of course, Jack reminded her of what Tom looked like on a daily basis and always had but that never triggered the bliss thing. No. That sparked a much softer sensation as she thought of a small boy worshipping his father as he grew up and the two of them getting closer and closer. Eventually being men together.

With a small sigh that acknowledged the complexity of what was happening in her life, Abby let something else trigger a release of that seemingly endless supply of bliss—the soft caress of a sea breeze on the bare skin of her arms, which made her think of a whisper of touch from Tom's lips.

'Are you happy, Mummy?' Jack asked. 'You're smiling again.'

'Mmm. I'm happy, hon.'

'Because we're going to Auckland?'

'I guess. It's a beautiful day for a ferry ride, isn't it?'

'I haven't seen a whale yet.'

'You might. We saw lots of dolphins, didn't we?'

Jack cupped his hands around his eyes to pretend they were binoculars but he couldn't keep his attention on the sea. 'Are we going to live in Auckland, Mummy?'

'No, hon. We're just going to visit for a day or two.'

'To see my *dad*.' Jack bounced up and down in excitement.

'Hold on to the rail,' Abby ordered, but she was still smiling. Despite repeated warnings to herself not to get her hopes up too high, she had to admit she was feeling more than a little bit of that excitement herself.

Or was it trepidation? Would Tom ask her to marry him again? And if he did, would he expect an answer this time? What could she tell him? That one night of bliss wasn't enough to turn her life upside down and hang her future on? Or, more importantly, Jack's life and future?

Not that she and Tom were likely to get any significant alone time. Just as they hadn't in the remainder of his visit after the night of Nathan's birthday party. It had been two weeks now since his volunteer stint had ended and he'd gone back to the mainland. The idea of marriage hadn't been raised again before he'd left, or since, in any text message or phone call. He was giving her space to think about what he'd said in the wake of their amazing night together, thanks to Jack's sleepover.

His words had hung in the darkness of her bedroom, almost shining with their intensity.

'I have to go back to Auckland soon, Abby. To my job. Like you said, there's nothing here for me on Kaimotu, career-wise.'

And there was everything for Abby and Jack. A home. A job. An amazing community.

'But I'm Jack's father and it's...it's incredible. *He's* incredible. I can't tell you how it makes me feel because I can't even describe it to myself but it's...it's huge, Abby.'

She had only been able to nod, her head brushing the side of Tom's chest, right beside his heart. She'd felt like that when she'd first held Jack as a baby, seconds after his birth. The world had changed for ever in that moment and her tears had been born from both amazement and joy.

'I want to be the best father I can be,' Tom had told her, and Abby had only been able to nod again.

Those tears at Jack's birth had held sadness, as well.

That there had been no father for her baby boy by her side to share the miracle. Guilt that she had been keeping this all for herself.

'I know it would be a big move for you and Jack to come to Auckland and it's too much to ask for right away but...I need to see Jack. As often as I can.'

And Jack needed to see his father. Abby had known that. She'd accepted it without question.

'Just come,' Tom had whispered into her ear as he'd held her close. 'Please. Even if it's only for a day or two.'

When Abby had booked the ferry tickets within days of Tom's departure, it had been his final words she'd kept hearing.

'Come soon. I'm going to miss you. *Both* of you.'

Jack's excitement only grew as the ferry moved through the Hauraki Gulf towards the sprawling city of Auckland.

'Look, Mummy. There's so many *boats*.'

'They're yachts, hon. See the sails? They call Auckland the "City of Sails" because so many people have yachts.'

'Does my dad have a yacht?'

'I don't know.'

'I'll ask him,' Jack said happily.

For the next few minutes they watched the pleasure crafts crowding the harbour waters and then the lovely harbour bridge as it drew steadily closer, but Abby wasn't really taking much notice.

She didn't know if Tom was into sailing. She didn't know anything about what his life away from work was like now. He was probably addicted to adventure sports like abseiling or parachuting. How would a child fit in with any of that?

What if he *did* have a yacht? Auckland had one of those 'four seasons in one day' types of climate. Tom could sail off with Jack on a lovely sunny morning and then a storm could blow in and they could end up in big trouble in the open sea and Jack could fall overboard and…and *drown*…

Oh, for God's sake. Abby gave herself a mental slap. Give him a chance, she told herself, without immediately envisaging a disaster.

Tom was meeting them off the ferry today. They would drop their bags at the motel where Abby and Jack were to stay the night and then they would have the rest of the day together.

Abby swallowed her concerns and smiled at Jack as he turned his imaginary binoculars onto her.

She would give Tom a chance. It was going to be interesting to see what he'd come up with for them to do today. More than interesting. Nerve-racking, because it was possible that three people's futures could be influenced in a major way by what happened today.

'Where are we going, Dad?'

'To the motel. To drop off your bags.'

'Why can't we stay at your house?'

'Because you need a bed of your own and my house is too small.' Tom had to avoid a sidelong glance to where Abby was sitting in the front passenger seat of his car. Abby wouldn't need a bed of her own. Damned frustrating to think of her sleeping in a motel tonight but he was treading slowly here. Carefully. Because of Jack.

She wouldn't even be here today if it wasn't about Jack spending some time with him, would she?

But it was *so* good to see her again.

He'd had his doubts. Of course he had.

There'd been a definite 'Oh, my God what was I *thinking*' moment when he'd stepped back into the familiar comfort of the house he shared with Moz and had realised that if he and Abby and Jack became a family, it would mean losing almost everything that was familiar and comfortable. That wave of…fear, almost, at the thought of such a different future had been thankfully receding a little more every day.

Even his long-held fear that having a family would somehow hold him back in his work was fading, too. He wasn't being any more cautious in what he did. If anything, he might be pushing the boundaries a tad further just to prove a point. He certainly didn't feel like his wings were being clipped in any way and yet there hadn't been a single day—a single hour, in fact—that he hadn't thought about Abby.

And Jack, of course. The relationships were very different but they were equally intense. Was one more important than the other?

Maybe the difference was that his relationship with Jack was simply there and all he had to do was make it as good as it could be. He was Jack's father and always would be.

A relationship with Abby, however, would have to be earned. And it might be harder to do that the second time around, because he had to try to undo the damage that had been done. When he'd made her feel like she wasn't as important as his career. That he didn't want her in his life because she would hold him back from being the person he wanted to be.

Whatever. It was important that they both have a good day today and Tom had given the matter a great deal of thought ever since Abby had texted to let him know she was bringing Jack to visit.

'Where are we going now?' Jack asked, as Tom drove them away from the motel.

'To the zoo.'

'What's a zoo?'

'Jack!' Abby sounded astonished. 'You know what a zoo is. Don't you?'

There was silence from the back seat.

'Jack?'

'I wanted Dad to tell me,' said a small voice.

Tom caught Abby's gaze and they shared a flash of something. Amusement tinged with apology on Abby's part and amusement mixed with maybe pride on Tom's part. It was something warm and adult that understood what was going on in a small boy's head. Something very poignant about Jack having to confess his attempt to connect with his father.

Tom shifted his gaze to the rear-view mirror so he could see Jack. 'Auckland zoo is special,' he told his son. 'It's been there for nearly a hundred years and it has hundreds of different sorts of animals and birds.'

'Has it got lions?'

'Yep.'

'And tigers?'

'Yep.'

'And monkeys?'

'Loads of monkeys. And chimpanzees and orang-utans and I'm not sure but there might be gorillas, too.'

'What else?'

'Have you ever seen a giant weta?'

'Ew...' Abby made a face. 'We get those at home. I'm not so keen on big bugs.'

'There's meerkats. There are people tunnels and you can climb through them and pop up into these Perspex bubbles and there you are, in the middle of the meerkat enclosure.'

'Oh, I'd love to do that.' Abby grinned. 'What do you think, Jack? Wouldn't that be fun?'

'Mmm. What else is there, Dad?'

'Have you ever seen a hippopotamus?'

'No-o-o...' Jack's eyes were round. 'I've never seen a hit...a hittopopamus.'

'Hippo-pot-amus,' Tom said slowly.

'Hitto-pop-amus,' Jack said, even more slowly.

'Close enough,' Tom said. His gaze slid sideways and this time there was pure amusement in the shared glance with Abby. The odd nerves that had been plaguing him about whether the zoo was the best idea for a day together disappeared completely.

This was going to be great.

Abby knew she'd never be able to decide what her favourite moment of this day had been because they were all so different and they each had their own magic.

Just walking along the miles of pathways, being parents and each holding the hand of the small boy between them, had been special.

'Swing,' Jack had commanded. 'Make me a *monkey*.'

And Tom and Abby would share a glance and mouth a silent count of three and then both lift Jack's feet off the ground in a big, forward swoop that made him shriek with delighted laughter.

The meerkats made them all laugh and shared laughter was absolutely the best, Abby decided.

Then again, the private, telepathic kind of laughter that passed between Tom and Abby with Jack's continued inability to pronounce 'hippopotamus' gave her heart an even more memorable squeeze.

And the bliss had been almost overwhelming when it had surfaced as she'd watched Tom eating an ice cream and catching a drip on the cone with his tongue. It had come supercharged with a hefty kick of desire, this time, thanks to the reality of his physical presence, and it had only got stronger as Abby had sensed the way he'd been watching *her* eat her ice cream.

Jack had been oblivious to the atmosphere above his head but Abby had barely noticed the alligators because she'd been concentrating so hard on trying to get her wayward thoughts under control.

In the end, however, there had really been only one moment that had stolen the limelight from them all, due to its significance.

They'd had afternoon tea at a café and had then wandered to a lovely grassy area near a band rotunda. Maybe they were all reluctant to head for an exit and finish their day at the zoo. The grass was long enough to be soft and tickly and there was a gentle slope under a tree that Jack spotted.

'Wanna see me do a roll, Dad? All the way down the hill?'

'Sure do.'

They both sat on the grass in the shade of the tree and watched Jack roll down the slope.

'I remember doing exactly the same thing when I was about his age,' Tom said with a note of wonder in his voice. 'It was a hell of a lot of fun.'

'Nothing to stop you doing it again,' Abby said with a grin.

Tom grinned right back. And then he simply turned sideways, lay down and started to roll, gathering speed fast.

'Look out, Jack, Dad's coming after you.' Abby had trouble shouting because she was laughing so hard.

But then Tom reached the bottom of the slope and rolled right into Jack and caught him in his arms, and her laughter died as she watched the rough and tumble between a father and his son as if it was an instinctual thing.

It was such a pure moment. A joyous moment.

Okay, there had to be a potential for Jack to get injured, but Abby wasn't thinking about any future catastrophe. She was absolutely in the moment and it felt utterly safe. Even if something *did* go wrong, Tom was here and he would look after them.

He would always look after them and keep them safe.

And Abby realised that she'd spent the whole day amongst wild animals. There'd even been a leopard or a cheetah or some big cat being walked around on a leash by a handler and not once today had she imagined something horrible happening.

Well, she'd thought about Tom's imaginary yacht and

Jack falling off and drowning but that had been before she'd been in Tom's company.

Before she'd felt so…safe.

Before she'd felt like she'd come home.

Yes, Abby knew perfectly well that there would be heartbreak if she lost Tom but if she didn't accept that future risk—something that might never actually happen—then she could never have this *now*.

And this now was absolutely perfect.

It was in this ultimately memorable moment that Abby gave Tom her heart.

Completely and for ever.

Even if they didn't end up being married or together as a family, it was too late to lock her heart up and constrict her life by trying to keep it safe. Her heart was Tom's. For better or worse, for richer or poorer. In sickness or health or even death.

He was her man just as decisively as Jack was her son.

Their son.

Her smile was misty as she watched Tom and Jack coming back up the hill on all fours, being tigers, maybe. Tom got to her first and flopped onto his side, propping his chin on his hand.

She was still smiling and Tom smiled back.

'Have I ever told you how gorgeous you are?'

He looked pretty gorgeous himself, with his hair all rumpled and bits of grass stuck in it. With his dark eyes still alight from the fun of the rough and tumble.

Or were they alight with something else?

They were so close. Abby could just lean forward and snatch a kiss. The sudden gleam in Tom's eyes suggested both his understanding and agreement and a tiny quirk of his lips was an irresistible invitation, but just as Abby tossed her braid over her shoulder so it wouldn't flop into Tom's face, a small human missile landed on top of him from the other side.

'*Gotcha.*'

'*Oof...*' Tom wrapped his hands around Jack's midriff and lifted him as if he weighed nothing. 'You sure did get me, buddy.'

Jack waved his arms and wriggled his legs but Tom's hand held him securely out of harm's way and then he tickled him and Jack shrieked with laughter and wriggled harder.

Abby could only laugh as well, tucking the disappointment over losing that kiss somewhere deep enough for it not to matter.

There was plenty of time.

Wasn't there?

Talk about bad timing.

Abby had been about to kiss him when that human missile had found its target.

Tom put Jack down and looked at his watch. 'If we head away now, we'd have time to drop into the rescue base. Would you like to see where I work, Jack?'

'*Yes.* Can I have a ride in a helicopter?'

'I'm not sure about that. Not today, anyway,' Tom added, as Jack's face fell. 'You could sit in one, though, and pretend you were driving.'

'Do I get a helmet?'

'I'm sure we can manage that.'

'Let's *go*.' Tom held out his hands to tug his parents from where they were still sitting on the grass.

So they went. Tom's crew was off duty but Moz was apparently there talking to a mechanic who had been called in to look at a helicopter. Frank was using the gym and Fizz was there, too, apparently watching Frank use the gym. Was there something going on that he didn't know about?

'Can't stay away from the place, can you? Fizz, this is Abby and this is Jack. My son. I told you about him.'

'Yeah…' Fizz grinned at Jack and then eyed Abby.

'Abby, this is my crew partner, Fizz.'

Abby eyed Fizz.

Frank caught Tom's eye and grinned. Both men could feel the wary vibe that had sparked instantly between the two young women.

'I'm working out,' Fizz said to Tom. 'See?' She opened her hand to show him a soft ball in her palm. 'Building up strength in my wrist.'

She was still wearing a protective bandage on her wrist, although the stitches were long gone and she'd been back on active duty for the last two weeks.

Jack's eyes were round. 'What happened to your hand?'

Fizz laughed, her gaze flicking towards Abby before moving to Tom. 'Your dad broke me.'

Tom cleared his throat—an annoyed sound. There were small ears here that might not detect a joke.

'Fizz hurt her arm when we were out on a job,' he told Jack.

'Yeah…' Fizz grinned at Jack again. 'We had to crawl into a crashed car at the bottom of a cliff with waves crashing around us. It was awesome. D'you want to be a helicopter paramedic when you grow up? Like Dad?'

'Yeah…' But Jack was biting his lip. He didn't sound confident, and why would he, when Fizz was making it sound so dangerous?

'Let's go and see a helicopter,' Tom said.

'The BK's out on a job,' Frank said. 'MVA up north. It'll be a while.'

'Backup's on site?'

'Yeah. The mechanic's going to have a look at that faulty fuel gauge. Moz is a bit worried it might be more than that.'

'They won't mind if Jack sits in the pilot's seat for a few minutes?'

'Might come and see how things are going myself.' Frank picked up a towel and mopped his face.

Fizz threw the soft ball into a bucket of hand weights. 'Me, too.'

The base manager was in the staffroom as they all trooped through.

'You must be young Jack,' he said. 'My word, you look like your dad, don't you?'

'Yep.' Jack stood on tiptoe to make himself taller. He stepped closer to Tom, who put his hand on his son's head.

He'd never felt so proud in his whole life.

'I'll bet you—' The base manager broke off his sentence as a signal announced an emergency radio message coming in. He moved swiftly towards his office and, with the door open, they could all hear as he picked up the microphone.

'Rescue Base One. Go ahead.'

'Rescue Base One, we have a priority one call from Kaimotu Island. I'll patch you through.'

Priority One meant a life-threatening emergency. They all knew that, apart from Jack, but the little boy went as still as everyone else as they listened. Could he feel the professional interest from Frank and Fizz? The alertness with which he himself was now listening? Or was it the flash of fear on his mother's face as she heard Ginny's familiar voice?

'Rescue One? We have a twenty-three-month-old boy, Blake Taggert, who's choking. Came in with a GCS of eight and deteriorating vital signs. Dr McMahon's tried to remove the obstacle with Magill forceps but without success. We're going to secure his airway with a cricothyroidectomy but we need urgent backup and evacuation.'

The base manager shook his head. 'Hold on.' He released the button so that Ginny couldn't hear him and turned towards Tom, looking rueful.

'It's a no-go for us. We'll have to see if the air force can help. It'll be an hour before the chopper's clear of that MVA and the backup's out of action.'

'They might not have started working on it yet. It's only a fuel gauge.'

'Kind of important when it's a distance that's pushing fuel capacity,' Frank reminded him.

'And it would be out of order,' the base manager snapped.

'I'd go with you.' Fizz had a sparkle in her eyes. An interesting mission with the added frisson of potential mechanical problems? She wanted in.

Was she crazy?

Was *he* crazy, even thinking about what he was thinking about?

Abby would think so. But when he caught her gaze, her eyes were shining, too. With tears.

'Poor Ruth,' she whispered. 'She must be frantic. Imagine if it was Jack and we were that far away from backup?'

That did it.

'I'll go,' Tom announced. 'If Moz is okay with the mission.' He was quite confident that the pilot would be prepared to take a small risk in a situation where a child's life was at stake. And the base manager might grumble and fuss but he'd find a way to bend the rules.

'Cool,' Fizz said.

'But no more crew,' Tom added. 'The less weight we have the less fuel we'll need so the gauge problem won't be such a major one.'

Tom left the base manager to update Ginny on what might be possible and moved swiftly towards the helipad. He knew Abby was following him. Any second now she would probably touch his arm and he'd stop and turn and have to see the plea in her eyes for him not to do something that must seem dodgy to someone who didn't know this business.

She wouldn't want him to risk his safety. For Jack's sake, now, as well as her own.

This was it. The crunch test of whether having Abby back in his life was going to mess with his career. A blinding flashback to the crux of why it hadn't worked the first time round.

Abby did touch his arm.

Tom did turn around.

But what he saw in her eyes wasn't fear. Not for him, anyway. It was fear for Ruth and Damien, parents of a small boy. An understanding of the agony they must be going through. An understanding of what only Tom could offer by way of help.

She hugged him goodbye swiftly, knowing she would have to get out of the way as preparations became fast and focused.

'Thank you,' was all she said. And then... 'I love you.'

That was when Tom kissed her.

Hard.

Right there on the helipad in front of everybody, including Jack. His words were far more private, however.

'See you soon, babe. I love you, too.'

CHAPTER TEN

IT WOULD BE HOURS before Tom returned.

There was the flight time to Kaimotu Island, the time needed to make sure little Blake was stable enough to travel, the trip back and then more time at the specialist paediatric hospital handing over his care before the chopper returned to base. There was probably a heap of paperwork that would need to be completed on top of that, especially given the protocols that must have been broken to send an aircraft out when it had been stood down for repairs.

Repairs that hadn't even been started.

Oh…help. It would be so easy to let her imagination conjure up a juicy disaster scene or three but Abby was determined not to go there. She wasn't going to let Jack see how worried she was.

They waved until the helicopter became no more than a speck in the distance and then Abby looked down to find Jack scowling up at her.

'Why are you *smiling*, Mummy?'

Was she? Abby touched the tip of a finger to the corner of her mouth and, yes, there was a faint tilt there.

Because, despite her worry, she was still singing

inside? Bathed in the glow that Tom's last words had given her?

I love you.

Were there any other little words in the universe that were that powerful?

Actually...maybe there were. Those four words *'I love you, too'* were more powerful because they confirmed something that was reciprocal. That brought people closer and cemented a relationship.

Her. And Tom. And Jack.

A real family.

So it was no wonder she was smiling a bit, was it? Not that Jack understood. Or approved.

'You shouldn't be happy,' he told his mother.

'Why not?'

'Because...' Jack sniffed. 'Because Dad's gone far away.'

'He'll be back soon.'

Jack's mouth turned down at the corners. 'He said we could have hamburgers and chips for dinner and that there was a big playground just for kids at the hamburger place. Will he be back in time to take us?'

'Hmm. Maybe not this time, hon.' Abby crouched down beside her son. 'But you might have to get used to things like this happening sometimes. It's what your daddy does. He's gone to rescue a very sick little boy. Brooke and Amber's little brother, Blake. Amber's in your class at school, isn't she? Imagine how sad she'd be if someone like your daddy *didn't* go and help make Blake better.'

Jack scowled harder but scuffed his foot thoughtfully, digesting Abby's words.

'Tell you what.' Abby straightened and took Jack's hand. They both needed distraction for a while, didn't they? 'Let's say goodbye to everybody here and how 'bout we get a taxi and go into the city? We can look at all the boats and find that hamburger restaurant and have dinner. Then we can go back to our motel and that way Dad will know where to find us. He might even be back in time to tuck you up and say goodnight.'

And then she and Tom would have some time alone.

Time to talk. To touch. To simply *be*.

Together.

Abby closed her eyes and blew out a long, long breath. The next few hours could well seem interminable.

They were. They were over an hour checking out all the yachts down at the viaduct and another hour watching Jack tucking into a hamburger and playing with a crowd of other children in the extensive indoor playground. By the time they arrived back at the motel it had been well over three hours since the helicopter had taken off from the rescue base.

More than enough time for it to have reached Kaimotu and for Blake to be on the way back. Was he all right? Had they needed the surgical intervention? Somebody would be able to tell her. With Jack happily splashing in the bath and playing boats with a plastic scrubbing brush, Abby picked up her mobile phone and made a call to Kaimotu Hospital.

'Ben.' She hadn't been expecting him to answer. 'How's Blake?'

'Crisis over, thank goodness. We're still monitoring

his breathing and he's obviously got a very sore throat but it's hardly surprising when you've tried to swallow a small, plastic aeroplane with sharp wings, is it?'

Ben's chuckle was wry but Abby was pushing away the cloud of relief to try and find what was ringing such a loud alarm bell in her mind. Was it because Ben knew what it was now that had caused the airway obstruction?

'You had to operate?'

'Not in the end. Once he was completely unconscious, there was no spasm to fight and I managed to get it out with the forceps. Not a moment too soon. Poor Ruth was beside herself.'

'I'll bet. Oh, I'm so glad to hear he's okay.' He must be more than okay if Tom had decided not to transfer him for follow-up.

The alarm bell rang louder.

'How long did it take for the chopper to get there?'

'We're still waiting,' came Ben's response. 'It hasn't shown up.'

It was Frank who answered Abby's call to the rescue base seconds later.

'I'm so sorry, Abby,' he said grimly. 'We don't know what's happened yet. All we know is that the chopper didn't make it to Kaimotu and it's not visible on radar. Last radio contact was two hours ago. A search plane's been dispatched.'

Abby felt curiously calm. It was probably the only benefit of a tendency to imagine the worst-case scenarios on an automatic basis. It meant that when they did happen, you didn't crumple up in shock because you'd been expecting them. You were ready.

'Can you call me, please?' Her voice only shook a little. 'Just as soon as you know anything?'

'Of course. Hang in there, Abby. Tom wouldn't give up without a bloody good fight. Especially now.'

Abby swallowed hard. 'Why especially now?'

Frank's voice was gentle. 'Because he's got so much to fight for, hasn't he?'

He meant Jack, Abby thought, as she ended the call. And...maybe me, too?

She did crumple then. Onto the couch, dropping the phone beside her so that she could bury her face in her hands.

She hadn't practised this scenario, had she? The one where she had to tell Jack that his daddy wasn't coming back.

Not tonight.

Not ever.

She'd thought about having to do it and the prospect had been horrific enough for her to keep Jack's existence a secret from his father.

Now her worst fear had been realised. No, it was worse than that. Jack had only just discovered his dad and fallen in love with him and now he was going to lose him. Thanks to her, he'd already lost all the years he could have had with his father in his life. How long would it be before her son could put those pieces of his life's jigsaw together and hate her for what she'd done?

She could see it now. He'd be maybe ten or eleven and he'd demand to know why he'd only had a few weeks of having a dad. He'd accuse Abby of—

Whoa. Why on earth was she doing this?

She didn't need to imagine a future disaster.

She had one happening right now.

Somehow she was going to have to tell Jack what had happened to Tom's helicopter.

To Tom.

Oh, God... The grief was pressing closer. She needed to get Jack into bed and sound asleep before that phone call came to confirm the worst. At least that way she'd have the rest of the night to try and find the best words to tell Jack.

And then they'd have to go home.

Only...Kaimotu Island would never really feel like home again, would it?

Home was where Tom was.

Didn't they say that you never really knew how precious something was until you lost it?

Well, they were right.

Tom had never given much thought to how precious his own life was until he was seriously contemplating the end of it.

As his helicopter spiralled down towards the ocean somewhere in the middle of nowhere, about halfway between New Zealand and Kaimotu Island.

Moz was swearing like a trooper. It wasn't just the fuel gauge that was faulty. Some major fault had wiped out so much they couldn't even send out a radio distress signal. They were just about to disappear off the radar and nobody would know why.

Except they would know why. This was happening because he'd put his hand up to take a risk. Pushed the boundaries like he always did, but this time he'd run out of luck.

And it wasn't just himself he was hurting. His best mate, Moz, was going down with him. And he was leaving the woman he loved behind.

Leaving the son he was only just getting to know.

Maybe he'd never stopped to think how precious his own life was because he'd never had that much to lose before. Maybe he'd avoided having that much to lose because then he'd be too aware of it and that was when you could start getting spooked. And then you couldn't do this kind of job as well as you might otherwise be able to.

Not that Tom had time to think about all that on the way down but there was plenty of time to think as they floated in their tiny emergency raft on that vast, icy ocean.

It was a miracle that they'd survived the crash. Even more of a miracle that a spotter plane had found them within hours and another rescue chopper could be scrambled to winch them out of the sea.

They had radio contact now. Had Abby been told they were safe and on their way home? That Blake had been airlifted from Kaimotu and was doing well in hospital on the mainland? Tom tried a patch from the helicopter to Abby's mobile phone but it rang and rang until he got voicemail.

He didn't want to leave a message.

He wanted to talk to Abby.

He *needed* to talk to her. So much that he couldn't go home to sleep when he and Moz had finally been checked out and then discharged, and had escaped from their base manager's relief disguised as anger over the foolhardiness he'd let them talk him into.

He had to go to Abby's motel and tap softly on the door, hoping that he would only wake her and not Jack, as well. That she wouldn't be too scared at having someone knocking on her door at some ungodly hour of the night.

The soft tapping on the door finally penetrated the numbness that Abby had wrapped around herself.

With her heart hammering, Abby got slowly to her feet. They'd sent someone to tell her in person, hadn't they? That was why she'd never received the phone call she'd been dreading so much.

She couldn't do this. Halfway to the door Abby stopped and had to stifle a sob with her fist. This was unbearable.

'Abby?' The voice was as soft as the knocking had been. 'Are you there?'

The voice was little more than a whisper but it was instantly recognisable. Abby could feel it slice through the numbness and bring every cell in her body back to life so intensely it was physically painful.

She threw herself at the door, fumbling with the lock in her haste to haul it open.

'Oh, my God…' she sobbed. 'You're still *alive*.'

And then Tom was through the door and filling the small space. Wrapping her in his arms and holding her so tightly her feet were off the floor and she couldn't take a breath but it didn't seem to matter because she'd never, *ever* been this happy.

Nothing was said for the longest time. They held each other very tightly and then Tom sank onto the couch with Abby still in his arms. She curled onto his lap with her arms still around his neck, gazing at his face as if she had to check that every pore of his skin was still intact. And then she had to touch and *feel* the reality of him. It was only then that their lips met in the gentlest kiss ever. The heartbreaking tenderness of that kiss sparked tears that rolled unheeded down Abby's face.

'I thought I'd lost you again,' she finally whispered. 'I…I've been sitting here for hours, wondering how on earth I was going to be able to tell Jack.'

'But they should have told you I was safe a long time ago. I tried to ring you myself from the chopper but all I got was voicemail.'

'What?' Abby blinked. 'But my phone was right beside me on this couch.'

They both looked for the phone but couldn't see it. Tom let go of her long enough to dig in the space between the cushions. He held up the phone and pressed a couple of buttons.

'It's been on silent,' he said. 'Looks like you've got a few voicemails here, babe.'

'Oh, no…' Abby groaned. 'And I've just been sitting here, imagining the worst when I didn't need to. That's the story of my life, isn't it? Imagining the worst and then avoiding it so it can't happen.'

'Like avoiding me, because I couldn't give you what you needed?'

'Not anymore.' Abby felt curiously shy as she met Tom's gaze. 'I realised today that it was too late.'

There was a flash of alarm in Tom's eyes now. 'Too late? You mean…for us?'

Abby wanted to smile but it didn't happen. Her lips wobbled instead. 'No…the opposite. Too late for me to try and keep my heart safe. It's yours, Tom. Whether or not you want it, it's yours. For ever.'

'Oh, I want it. You can't begin to know how much.' He pressed another of those exquisitely tender kisses on her lips and then tucked Abby's head against his shoulder, resting his cheek on her hair.

She was pressed against his heart. She could feel its steady beat right through her body. Could feel her own heart rate slowing a little until the beats matched.

'I realised something, too,' he said softly. 'It made more sense today but I realised it a while back. When we all got out of that mine safely.'

Abby felt his chest swell as he took a deep breath. For a moment she couldn't feel his heartbeat so clearly and then his ribs sank again and she could feel that comforting thud and her own breath came out in a contented sigh.

'I've spent my whole life chasing danger,' Tom went on. 'Because I thought that was what made life worth living. Not the danger itself but that rush of feeling safe afterwards. I never knew how wrong I'd got it all. Until I met you and even then I didn't understand.'

Abby was puzzled. She tilted her head, trying to find the answer in Tom's face, but he just smiled at her.

'I always went for women who were just as crazy as me.'

Abby's heart skipped a beat. 'Women like Fizz?'

A tiny nod. 'And you were the absolute opposite. So safety conscious. I thought that you would stop me chasing danger and getting that feeling that life was so worth living afterwards.'

'I don't want to do that.' Abby pushed herself to sit

upright so that she could make sure Tom understood properly. 'I never want to do that. I know I'm not as brave as someone like Fizz but—'

Tom stopped her rush of words with a gentle finger on her lips. 'Shh...' He was shaking his head. 'Let me finish.'

Abby shushed.

'The thing that I realised properly today is that it isn't where the feeling comes from. An adrenaline rush might make you *feel* more alive for a while but what makes life worth living is *this*...'

He kissed her again. And again.

'I love you so much, Abby. You make every breath worth taking. You *are* my life. You and Jack. You're my people. My family.'

As if on cue, a small, sleepy figure in a pair of pyjamas patterned with bright green dinosaurs stumbled through the door of the motel's tiny living area, his Action Man doll dangling head down from one hand.

Jack blinked. And then he smiled.

'Hi, Dad,' he said. 'You came home.'

'Yeah...' Tom's voice sounded a bit choked. He held one arm out to invite Jack closer for a cuddle but then his gaze caught Abby's and held it as he tugged her closer as well.

'I came home,' was all he said.

It was all he needed to say. They were finally together. A family. And Abby knew they would stay that way and she would make the most of every single minute of it.

Home.

Maybe that was the most powerful word in the universe. Jack's sleepy feet had brought him close enough to be scooped up by Tom to join Abby on his lap. She put an arm around her precious son, as well. It was a tangle of arms and she ignored the painful poke from the foot of the plastic doll. This was a squeezy hug to end all squeezy hugs.

Because it was their first family hug. Abby knew with absolute certainty that it would be the first of a countless number. That, maybe, in the not-too-distant future, there would be even more of a tangle of small limbs and plastic toys to contend with.

Somehow, over the top of Jack's tousled curls, Tom managed to find Abby's lips for a kiss just for her.

'Marry me?' he whispered.

Abby could only nod, her heart too full for her head to find words. It wasn't much of an answer to a proposal, was it?

She'd kiss him again, she decided. Properly. Just as soon as they'd tucked their son back into bed.

* * * * *

Mills & Boon® Hardback
August 2013

ROMANCE

The Billionaire's Trophy	Lynne Graham
Prince of Secrets	Lucy Monroe
A Royal Without Rules	Caitlin Crews
A Deal with Di Capua	Cathy Williams
Imprisoned by a Vow	Annie West
Duty At What Cost?	Michelle Conder
The Rings that Bind	Michelle Smart
An Inheritance of Shame	Kate Hewitt
Faking It to Making It	Ally Blake
Girl Least Likely to Marry	Amy Andrews
The Cowboy She Couldn't Forget	Patricia Thayer
A Marriage Made in Italy	Rebecca Winters
Miracle in Bellaroo Creek	Barbara Hannay
The Courage To Say Yes	Barbara Wallace
All Bets Are On	Charlotte Phillips
Last-Minute Bridesmaid	Nina Harrington
Daring to Date Dr Celebrity	Emily Forbes
Resisting the New Doc In Town	Lucy Clark

MEDICAL

Miracle on Kaimotu Island	Marion Lennox
Always the Hero	Alison Roberts
The Maverick Doctor and Miss Prim	Scarlet Wilson
About That Night...	Scarlet Wilson

0713 GEN STD HB

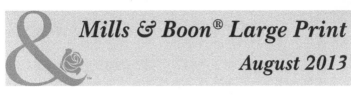

Mills & Boon® Large Print
August 2013

ROMANCE

Master of her Virtue	Miranda Lee
The Cost of her Innocence	Jacqueline Baird
A Taste of the Forbidden	Carole Mortimer
Count Valieri's Prisoner	Sara Craven
The Merciless Travis Wilde	Sandra Marton
A Game with One Winner	Lynn Raye Harris
Heir to a Desert Legacy	Maisey Yates
Sparks Fly with the Billionaire	Marion Lennox
A Daddy for Her Sons	Raye Morgan
Along Came Twins...	Rebecca Winters
An Accidental Family	Ami Weaver

HISTORICAL

The Dissolute Duke	Sophia James
His Unusual Governess	Anne Herries
An Ideal Husband?	Michelle Styles
At the Highlander's Mercy	Terri Brisbin
The Rake to Redeem Her	Julia Justiss

MEDICAL

The Brooding Doc's Redemption	Kate Hardy
An Inescapable Temptation	Scarlet Wilson
Revealing The Real Dr Robinson	Dianne Drake
The Rebel and Miss Jones	Annie Claydon
The Son that Changed his Life	Jennifer Taylor
Swallowbrook's Wedding of the Year	Abigail Gordon

Mills & Boon® Hardback
September 2013

ROMANCE

Challenging Dante	Lynne Graham
Captivated by Her Innocence	Kim Lawrence
Lost to the Desert Warrior	Sarah Morgan
His Unexpected Legacy	Chantelle Shaw
Never Say No to a Caffarelli	Melanie Milburne
His Ring Is Not Enough	Maisey Yates
A Reputation to Uphold	Victoria Parker
A Whisper of Disgrace	Sharon Kendrick
If You Can't Stand the Heat...	Joss Wood
Maid of Dishonour	Heidi Rice
Bound by a Baby	Kate Hardy
In the Line of Duty	Ami Weaver
Patchwork Family in the Outback	Soraya Lane
Stranded with the Tycoon	Sophie Pembroke
The Rebound Guy	Fiona Harper
Greek for Beginners	Jackie Braun
A Child to Heal Their Hearts	Dianne Drake
Sheltered by Her Top-Notch Boss	Joanna Neil

MEDICAL

The Wife He Never Forgot	Anne Fraser
The Lone Wolf's Craving	Tina Beckett
Re-awakening His Shy Nurse	Annie Claydon
Safe in His Hands	Amy Ruttan

ROMANCE

A Rich Man's Whim	Lynne Graham
A Price Worth Paying?	Trish Morey
A Touch of Notoriety	Carole Mortimer
The Secret Casella Baby	Cathy Williams
Maid for Montero	Kim Lawrence
Captive in his Castle	Chantelle Shaw
Heir to a Dark Inheritance	Maisey Yates
Anything but Vanilla...	Liz Fielding
A Father for Her Triplets	Susan Meier
Second Chance with the Rebel	Cara Colter
First Comes Baby...	Michelle Douglas

HISTORICAL

The Greatest of Sins	Christine Merrill
Tarnished Amongst the Ton	Louise Allen
The Beauty Within	Marguerite Kaye
The Devil Claims a Wife	Helen Dickson
The Scarred Earl	Elizabeth Beacon

MEDICAL

NYC Angels: Redeeming The Playboy	Carol Marinelli
NYC Angels: Heiress's Baby Scandal	Janice Lynn
St Piran's: The Wedding!	Alison Roberts
Sydney Harbour Hospital: Evie's Bombshell	Amy Andrews
The Prince Who Charmed Her	Fiona McArthur
His Hidden American Beauty	Connie Cox